SILENT STRANGER

Silent Stranger

Paula F. Winskye

AONIAN PRESS
JAMES A. ROCK & COMPANY, PUBLISHERS
FLORENCE • SOUTH CAROLINA

Silent Stranger by Paula F. Winskye

(*Aonian Press*)

is an imprint of JAMES A. ROCK & CO., PUBLISHERS

Address comments and inquiries to:

AONIAN PRESS
James A. Rock & Company, Publishers
900 South Irby Street, #508
Florence, SC 29501
E-mail:
jrock@rockpublishing.com   lrock@rockpublishing.com
Internet URL: www.rockpublishing.com

ISBN: 978-1-59663-744-3

Library of Congress Control Number: 2009923695

Printed in the United States of America

First Edition: 2009

For my dad
James A. Pfeiffer, (1909-1975)
a World War II veteran, part of the
first Army unit on Guadalcanal,
wounded on Bougainville.
A horseman and lifelong farmer, my
love of horses comes from him.

And my mom
Vivian F. Pfeiffer.
She has given so much for all her
children. I am grateful for her love
and support through the years.

Both my parents gave me
the greatest gift of all.
Faith in God.
Thank you.

I.

Michelle Bowman pulled her brown hair into a ponytail. Outside her kitchen window, a cloudless sky provided the perfect backdrop for the ranch yard and the mountains beyond. The rainy, spring weather had finally broken.

"Good day for a field trip."

She called the mothers of her six students, her sisters-in-law, and asked them to pack lunches. Usually the kids ate at home, a duplex across the yard, while Michelle used the time to correct papers.

She stowed her own lunch and other supplies in a backpack, then laced her hiking boots. After loading her Winchester 3030 rifle, she checked the safety. Having spent her entire life in these mountains, the rifle seemed as natural as her boots. The kids raced up the walk while she pulled on her backpack.

"Where we going, Michelle?" Matt, the oldest at twelve, asked.

"I thought we'd try for Cougar Rock." She smiled at their delight. Cougar Rock meant a whole day away from the classroom. She slung the rifle over her shoulder. "Matt, take up the rear."

"Again?"

Michelle frowned.

"You know why."

Matt nodded. Following the trail past her parents' house, she picked a fern in the woods and asked them to identify the species. They crossed the still-flooding creek on a bridge her grandfather had built. The trail began climbing almost immediately.

Michelle set her pace according to the capability of her youngest student, Tim, seven. Frequent stops to teach science gave them a breather.

"Plant species change as much when we climb a hundred feet as they would if we traveled a hundred miles ... See how the heavy rain has eroded the soil up here. All the good soil washes into the valley. That's why your great-grandfather built his ranch there."

The kids identified bird species and collected minerals. During a rest stop, Matt shouted.

"Hey, look! A cougar track!"

"Is not!" ten-year-old Sara said.

"Is too!"

"Let me see," Michelle leaned over, examining a patch of mud, no bigger than a baseball, filling a depression in the rock. It contained part of a footprint with three toes. "Well, I'm not sure what it is, but it's not a cougar. Remember, Matt, a cat's toes are farther apart at the end than at the base."

"Oh. Yeah. But it's too big for a wolf. What is it?"

"We can't see enough of the track to say. It could even be a small bear. His claws would have touched the rock and not made a mark in the mud."

"Maybe it's a big foot."

"Pretty small for a big foot."

"A baby big foot?"

"Nice try. You lead the way for a while."

He grinned, the unexpected honor making him forget the track. But Michelle could not forget. It looked more human than animal.

At a place with a panoramic view, she quizzed the kids about the names of the surrounding peaks. They watched an eagle soar below before hiking on.

She stopped for lunch at the Stadium, an expanse of granite the size of a football field with no overhanging cliffs and little cover for predators. Boulders provided chairs. When they finished eating, she told her students to use their backpacks for pillows and take a nap. Although the older students did not need it, they cooperated for the sake of their younger siblings.

Michelle, rifle in hand, wandered the edges of the granite where larger boulders and gnarled trees promised something with which she could interest her students. She decided to explain that these were the same species as the magnificent trees around the ranch buildings.

She froze, staring at the patch of mud. This time she could see the whole print. The whole *human footprint*. She placed her foot beside the track. A little bigger than her boot. A man's track.

How could anyone walk around barefoot at this time of year? She searched for any distinguishing features and found none. *It rained hard last night. He left this track today.* She repositioned the 3030 and surveyed the area. Nothing moved.

"Whatcha looking at?" Sara asked, much too close.

Michelle turned, destroying the track with her boot.

"Just looking. Let's wake the kids and head back."

"But we were going to Cougar Rock."

"I don't think Jeff and Tim can make it there and back. We don't want to carry them part way home."

Sara agreed, as did Matt, having carried tired siblings on other occasions. Michelle let Sara lead while she kept vigil with her rifle. Before she descended the trail, she dropped some snack bars at the spot where they had eaten lunch.

For several minutes, nothing moved on the rock.

Then a disheveled, emaciated figure emerged from the boulders. His filthy feet carried him lightly across the rock. He grabbed the bars and scurried back to cover. His eyes darted about while he tore open the wrappers and stuffed the food into his mouth.

A dark beard could not hide his hollow cheeks and anyone could count his ribs because no shirt covered them. Jeans, which may have fit at one time, stayed up only because a length of rope held them in place.

He licked the inside of each wrapper and studied the spot where Michelle and the children had disappeared. Finally, he followed.

II.

During the return trip, Michelle carried on an internal debate. Should she tell her family about a barefoot man in the mountains? *Yes! He could be dangerous!* But she knew how her father and brothers would react. *They'll pack guns like this is the old west.*

This guy's probably starving and scared. That first track wasn't far from the ranch. If he wanted to attack somebody, he already would have.

By the time they reached the ranch, she had decided to delay informing her family. She dismissed her students for the weekend, unloaded her rifle, then visited both her mother and sisters-in-law.

Michelle returned to the classroom in her house to prepare a quiz on plant species. She worked at her desk, but her eyes wandered to the window.

Something doesn't look right. But what? She studied the shelf sitting in front of the window. *Is something missing? The jar of fruit snacks.*

"Those kids."

They had pilfered the snacks. The shelf stood right next to the door. *They wouldn't even have to step inside.* But she thought again. The kids would have tried not to take so many that she noticed. And they certainly would have left the jar.

Her chest tightened as she walked to the screen door and studied the empty playground. Thick trees surrounded it. She opened the door, hesitated, then descended the two steps, surveying the flower beds on either side.

A bare footprint, deep in the mud, as if someone had jumped off the steps in flight. Michelle shuddered, rubbed out the print, and returned to the classroom, locking the door.

Again, she vowed not to tell anyone. This man *must* be starving, lost, and scared. She needed to help him, without taking unnecessary risks. *I'll leave something more substantial on the playground tonight.*

* * *

The next morning, the sandwiches and fruit had disappeared, the snack jar left in their place.

Michelle declined her mother's invitation to go on the weekly fifty-mile trip to town. Nothing unusual. She liked the solitude of the ranch.

After placing more food on the playground, she sat on a child's chair and watched over the classroom windowsill. An hour passed. Her legs cramped. She considered giving up her vigil.

Then the brush stirred. She held her breath, but nearly groaned when she saw him. *How can he still be walking? He must have an amazing will to live.* Despite her fear, she wanted to bring him into her home and feed him back to health. But his every action told her that he would flee.

He did not eat where she left the food. He retreated to the edge of the brush, his eyes darting about. He stopped chewing frequently to listen.

She tried to memorize his features. Dark hair, almost black, and a full beard, neither of which had been trimmed in some time. No shirt. Filth. She thought he wore jeans, but could not be sure under all that dirt. His race? Not black. But maybe not white either. Age? Maybe middle aged? His hair had not turned gray.

When he finished, he returned the containers and disappeared into the woods.

He's more afraid of me than I am of him. And that isn't easy. Two questions plagued her most. *How? Why?* No one deserved to live like that.

* * *

"I can't keep feeding him on the playground. The kids will notice," Michelle said to herself.

She knew of a safer place, just a hundred yards up the slope behind her house. She shuddered. *That means going into the woods with a strange man.* She could carry her rifle, but that might frighten him.

She opened her top dresser drawer and pulled out the pepper spray. It had kept her feeling safe enough to finish college. She smiled.

"Courage in a bottle."

Jamming the canister into her back pocket, she gathered food, a bottle of juice, an old blanket, and an over-sized sweatshirt. While crossing the playground, the hair bristled on the back of her neck.

"C-c-come on, stranger."

She climbed the hill to the rock outcrop with its shallow grotto. After depositing her bundle twenty yards from the rock, she grasped the pepper spray with a trembling hand and entered the grotto. She waited on a boulder with her back to the wall.

Twenty minutes passed. Again, she saw branches move before he emerged. They stared at each other, both in "fight or flight" mode, for several minutes more. He eased toward the food and crouched to eat, never taking his eyes off her.

Michelle fought it as long as she could. But finally, she had to let the sneeze out. He jumped backward, wide-eyed, nearly falling. But after only a minute, he finished eating. He looked under the sweatshirt and blanket.

"You want more food?" He cringed again. "You need to get used to my voice. And maybe talking will keep me from freaking out. Can you understand me? You can sure hear me."

He gazed at her. Michelle stood and he backed away.

"Don't go. I won't hurt you. I feel a little cornered in here."

They circled each other. He stopped near the rock face at the edge of the trees. She picked up the sweatshirt and held it up to herself.

"See. It's a shirt. It's warm. It'll fit you."

She extended it toward him. He watched, holding his ground. Michelle advanced step by step. He straightened. His muscles tightened. She stretched her arm as far as she could.

He snatched the shirt from her. She eased backward until he ignored her. He hugged the sweatshirt and sighed.

"Put it on." He did not move. Michelle pulled her sweatshirt off, then replaced it. "Like that."

He studied the garment. After some maneuvering, he pulled it over his head. He stroked the soft material.

"Feels pretty good doesn't it." She opened the blanket and approached him again. "You're not as scared as you were. Wish I could trust you that fast." He took the blanket. "I'll bring you more food this evening."

* * *

For the next week, she fed him daily before and after school. He ate every crumb and looked for more. He progressed to taking the food from her hand.

"If you get much more comfortable with me, I'll run home screaming. I think you're harmless. Unfortunately, that doesn't matter. You're a man. And any man over age fifteen scares me to death. Don't get me wrong. I'm getting more comfortable with you. I haven't even taken the pepper spray out of my pocket for three days."

He wolfed his food, ignoring her speech. She wrinkled her nose.

"You really need a bath. And better care than I can give you out here. Besides, sooner or later somebody's going to notice how fast my food's disappearing. I need to tell my family about you. Dad's going to flip. But I think I can convince him you're not dangerous. I hope."

She let out a soft whistle. He raised his head for an instant, then continued eating. When he had devoured every morsel, he set the containers aside. He started toward her twice, extending his hand, then withdrawing it.

Michelle tensed, her eyes on his hand—dirt under every nail and in every crack. He again reached for her, this time briefly touching her cheek. Then he retreated. She wiped tears away.

"What happened to you? Why can't you talk? Or understand me? Somebody must miss you. I read the news. I haven't heard anything about a missing person your age." She paused. "I can't even tell how old you are. Maybe fifty. I need to clean you up, cut your hair, and shave that beard so we can see what you look like."

She rose.

"I'd better go."

He followed her almost to the playground. But when they heard the kids on the swings, he disappeared. Michelle said a prayer of thanks. Better that he avoided the rest of the family until she broke the news.

III.

Sunday morning, before Michelle walked to her parents' house to listen to a church service, she delivered more food to her guest. After dinner, she would tell her father everything.

While they cleared the table, the dogs began barking.

"Sounds like they got something treed," Les Bowman said. "Boys, get the guns. The rest of you, stay in the house."

Michelle felt a knot in her stomach and ignored her father's words, afraid she knew what the dogs had cornered in a cul-de-sac created by the barn and a storm fence. Her brother, Chris glanced over his shoulder.

"What're you doing here?"

"You might need me."

"Huh?"

They hurried until the trapped animal came into view. Michelle's guest.

"Oh, no," she said.

"My God," Les murmured. "He's a walking skeleton." When the man saw them, his eyes widened and he tried to climb the twelve-foot wall. One of the dogs seized the opening and grabbed his leg. "Ruff, heel! Bo, heel! I don't care if he's a stranger, you don't attack a person!"

The dogs obeyed, moving behind Les. The wild man tried to

climb the wall again, only succeeding in opening wounds on his hands and arms.

"You're scaring him," Michelle said.

"Then we're even, because he's scaring the heck out of me. I thought I told you to stay in the house."

"I thought you'd need me if it was him. I've been feeding him for a week."

"You *what?*"

"He's starving."

"You knew he was hanging around the ranch and you didn't say anything?"

"I was afraid you'd react this way."

"With good reason!"

"You two want to quit jawing so we can decide what to do about him?" Chris said. "Terry and I can catch him no problem, but then what?"

"No," Michelle insisted. "He's been through enough already. He needs to learn that he can trust us. Let me see if I can get close to him." All three Bowman men began to argue, but Michelle stepped forward. "Lower your guns."

Les tried to protest, but Michelle gave him a look.

"Where'd that courage come from?"

"I've had a week with him, Dad. He won't hurt me."

"Okay. Give it a try. But he's acting like an animal, honey. A cornered animal can attack."

"Then back up. Take the pressure off him."

They took a few steps back while she advanced. The wild man's arms dropped to his sides and his eyes focused on her. She saw suspicion, but he did not retreat. She whispered.

"You know I won't hurt you. Let me help you. You need more than food."

She stretched her hand toward him. Another three feet and she could touch him. He backed away. Michelle dropped to her knees, to appear non-threatening. He inched toward her, briefly touched her hand, then withdrew. She remained immobile for so long that her arm began shaking. He approached again. This time he did not pull back.

She rose and moved closer, stroking his coarse, greasy hair, trying to ignore the stench.

"Back up. Let him see that he's free to go."

"We can't let him go," Les said.

"We have to. He needs to stay here because he wants to. We can't help him if we have to keep him locked up."

After some grumbling, the men obeyed. Michelle took his hand and led him to the opening. Seeing freedom, he pulled away and ran to the end of the barn. He stopped and looked back. She gestured for him to come, to no avail. She walked toward her house, urging him to follow.

Just before she lost sight of him, he moved, staying about fifty yards to the side and fifty yards back. Her father and brothers paralleled him, leaving enough distance to keep him comfortable. Michelle settled into a chair on her porch, then watched him work his way around the yard until he sat on the side of her porch, his back against the wall, watching the men.

"Bev," Les called. "Bring him something to eat. The rest of you, stay put."

When Bev brought roast beef sandwiches and a slice of pie, the stranger tensed. But his hunger outweighed his fear. He grabbed the plate, eating even the pie with his hands, ignoring the fork.

"Oh, Michelle. The poor thing. We need to clean him up and treat his wounds."

"How?"

"The kids' pool. We'll hook a hose to your kitchen sink. I'll get the supplies."

"Let him relax a while longer. He's had a rough day."

"Okay. But I'll collect the stuff."

"Bring a garbage bag for his clothes."

"They can go right in the burn barrel."

"No. They might have clues to help identify him."

"Right. We'll need all the help we can get. I'll bring some rubber gloves too."

The wild man stayed on Michelle's porch until his head began to nod. When he disappeared into the woods, she felt anxious. She busied herself preparing more food for him, then waited on the porch. An hour later, he returned and devoured the food.

Bev had been watching from the ranch house. She wandered over and began filling the pool with warm water. The wild man studied the operation, then walked to the pool and felt the water before rubbing it up his arms. Bev handed him a bar of soap and he washed with enthusiasm.

"He doesn't like his condition any more than we do," Michelle said.

"See if you can get him out of those jeans and into the water."

With a gloved hand, Michelle tugged at the waist of his jeans. He slid them off without untying the rope.

"Ew-w!" Bev picked them up with two fingers and dropped them into a garbage bag.

Michelle pulled on his hand and he stepped into the tub, sitting down to continue his bath. She eased the hose up to his head. His hair shed water.

"He's certainly not shy."

"Even less than most men."

Michelle lathered his hair.

"How old do you think he is?"

"Maybe fifty."

"It's beginning to look like he's Caucasian. What's this mark on his neck?"

"There's one on the other side too." Bev examined it. "Looks almost like an old burn. What happened to this poor man? Why doesn't he talk? Maybe he's a foreigner."

"Habla Español?" No response. "Parlez-vous Français?" He continued bathing. "He's not deaf. Maybe he can't speak."

"He might be an escaped mental patient."

"I guess anything's possible."

She rinsed the soap from his hair and beard and began scrubbing his back.

"What's this?"

Lines cris-crossed his back. Bev studied the marks and gasped.

"Michelle, this man's been beaten."

Michelle continued washing him, trying to keep her back to Bev to hide her tears. In the process, she noticed his now-clean arms and chest.

"Mom, what are these round marks?"

After a silent moment, Bev stroked his hair.

"Poor, baby. Who hated you so much that they hurt you this way? No wonder you can't talk. I saw a mark like that once. He has dozens. Those are cigarette burns."

Michelle looked at her mother and saw tears.

"We have to protect him. We can't let anyone hurt him again. We can do that, can't we?"

"Honey, we have no right. Your dad already called Frank. He probably has a family who is worried sick about him."

"But until they find his family, we can take care of him. We can't let them lock him up in some hospital. He doesn't like feeling cornered."

"Michelle, he's not a stray dog. He's a man. He may be weak now, but what happens when he starts feeling better? What happens when he notices that you're a woman?"

Michelle hesitated.

"I'll be careful. I'll lock my doors and we'll put a mattress on the porch for him. Like you said, they'll find his family. Then they can decide what to do with him. But let's just take care of him until then."

"I'll talk to your dad."

Bev wiped her wrist across her eyes. "He has bed sores from sleeping on the ground with those bony joints. I think he's clean.

I'll bring a chair. You try to get the snarls out while I treat his wounds."

"It would be easier if I just cut his hair."

"Let's hold off giving him access to sharp objects."

Michelle tugged on his hand and he climbed out of the pool. When she handed him a towel, he dried himself. For the first time, she noticed that he stood at least six feet. Bev brought the chair and he sank into it.

"I think he's tired," Michelle said.

"He doesn't have a lot of energy reserve and he's had a rough day." She turned to her husband and sons, who had brought chairs to the edge of Michelle's lawn. "Can one of you get a mattress, pillow, and sleeping bag from the motor home? We'll make a bed for him on Michelle's porch."

Bev squirted peroxide into the sore on his shoulder. He sprang from the chair, away from her, then faced her, snarling.

"Bev, get back!" Les shouted.

"Dad, calm down," Michelle said. She soothed the man, but he would not return to the chair until Bev moved away. Michelle extended her hand. "I'd better do it."

Bev frowned.

"Maybe you'd better not."

Michelle removed her glove.

"I have a cut on my hand. I'll show him that it hurts, but we need to do it."

She squirted peroxide on her cut and mugged to make it clear that it hurt. She handed the peroxide to him and pointed at his wounds. He cleaned them himself, hardly wincing for any but the one on his right hip. She placed antiseptic on her finger, then offered it to him. Again, he treated himself. After she bandaged her finger, he allowed her to bandage his wounds.

Bev marveled.

"We shouldn't be surprised. You're good with kids and animals. Now get some clothes on him. I'll get his bed from Chris."

"Mom, look at his waist. Is that a tan line?"

"I think so. Nobody in Wyoming has a tan line this time of year."

"He must come from the south. He has a tattoo on his left shoulder. A sore's hiding part of it, but I can make out red inside a circle."

"That should help identify him."

He dressed in the T-shirt and sweat pants Michelle handed him. Before she offered him moccasins, she rubbed lotion on his abused feet and trimmed his toenails. She gave him the nail clipper. When he just stared at it, she helped him cut the first fingernail. He gazed at her. She guided him with the second. After a puzzled moment, he finished the job.

"He knows how to take care of himself. Or, at least he used to."

"That'll make our job easier. Let's see if he'll bed down for a nap."

Michelle sat on the porch and he occupied the mattress. He could not resist sleep for long. When she walked away to talk to her father, Les whistled.

"You have a way with him. Frank was just going to a car accident when I called him. He'll be here later. He's having a heck of a Sunday afternoon."

"Tell Frank he's staying here until they can find his family."

"No way! We can't ..."

"Don't bother, Les," Bev said. "We've already had this argument. He'll do better here than in some hospital. Michelle will keep her door locked."

Les growled.

"And one of us men will sit here with a gun during the day. It's not just you, Michelle. The kids have to come over here. How'll he react to that?"

"They're small. He won't feel threatened. He'll sense their compassion."

"We'll see."

IV.

When Sheriff Frank Owens drove into the yard, Michelle's guest woke and ran around the corner of her house. She coaxed him back and used the sheriff's camera to take pictures while Frank stayed just off the lawn.

"I need his finger prints and DNA too," Frank said, grinning.

"Of course. Do you have evidence bags?"

"Course."

"Give me one."

She polished a glass, filled it with water, then holding it with her fingertips, offered it to her guest. He emptied the glass. When she opened the evidence bag, he dropped it in. Frank chuckled when she brought it to him.

"And DNA?"

She pulled a brush from her pocket.

"Will hair follicles do? I got plenty trying to unsnarl that bird's nest."

"Just fine."

"What else do you need? I took pictures of his tattoo. The scars too, but I don't think any description of him will mention those."

"Your dad says someone tortured him."

"He was beaten and burned with cigarettes."

"I hope it didn't happen around here. I'd hate to think someone I know could be that sadistic."

Michelle shuddered.

"Yeah. Dad, did you give Frank his clothes? Maybe they can tell us where he's been."

"Yeah. Frank, what you think about us taking care of him until you figure out who he is?"

"It'd sure save me a lot of trouble and paperwork. I have the final word until we put a name to him. He seems pretty healthy for his condition. But if that changes, you call right now. If he gets sick, he has to go to a hospital."

"Right. But maybe he's not in this condition because he's starving. He could have some disease. Shouldn't you run some tests on him?"

"Good idea. I suppose I'd have to bring somebody out here to draw blood. Michelle, will he let somebody poke him with a needle?"

"Well, maybe. When we treated his wounds, it didn't bother him when I treated my own first. If the lab tech poked me first. I really hate needles."

"But you'll do it."

"Yeah. I guess so. Bring a female lab tech. He's not as afraid of women."

"Good idea. You got something in your EMT kit in case he has an allergic reaction?"

"Of course. After Dr. Page sees the lab results, maybe he could call me with some advice on nutrition."

"I'll talk to him. I'll get this description out today and I'll be back tomorrow. If we don't get a match right away, I'll have you e-mail updated pictures. His own mother probably wouldn't recognize him now."

***

"Why can't he talk?" Tim asked.

Michelle had made the man her class project for the day. He accepted the children just as she had expected.

"We don't know for sure. But we think something very bad happened to him."

"Did he get so scared that he can't talk?" Keith said.

"Something like that. His brain just couldn't handle what happened, so it said, I'm leaving for a while until things get better."

"But things are better now."

"That's the problem. Sometimes it doesn't know that it's safe to come back."

"Won't his brain ever come back?"

"No one knows."

"How can we help him?" Sara asked.

"We can be his friends and try hard not to scare him. We can make him part of our school. He's really thin. We'll see how tall he is and weigh him every day. Tim and Keith will keep track of his weight. Jill and Sammy, you write down everything he eats and every so often, we'll figure out how many calories he's eating. Matt and Sara, your job will be keeping track of his body mass index. As he gains weight, we'll calculate percentages."

"Let's take pictures of him too," Sara said. "So we can remember how bad he looked."

"Well, let's say so we can see how much better he looks."

"He doesn't like that beard," Matt said. "He keeps scratching it."

"I'll give him a shave and a haircut."

When she entered the house for supplies, the man looked after her, shifting from one foot to the other. Tim took his hand.

"Don't worry. She'll come back."

Michelle brought the scale to the porch and had him stand on it.

"Keith, how much does he weigh?"

"One hundred ... twenty-five. That's a lot."

"Is it? When you go home for lunch, ask your dads what they weigh. Let's ask Grandpa what he weighs."

"Yeah," Matt said. "Grandpa, how much do you weigh?"

Les answered from his lawn chair in the shade.

"Why you want to know?"

"He only weighs one, twenty-five."

"I weigh more than that."

"Just tell them, Dad," Michelle said.

"Two, thirty."

The kids marveled while she seated her guest and began hacking off his hair.

"Have you ever cut hair?" Sara asked.

"No. But anything should be an improvement."

She trimmed the back even with his hair line, then tried to layer it. By the time she reached the front, she had refined her technique enough not to make a liar of her. Her guest relaxed and gave a contented sigh.

"He likes the attention," Jill said.

"I'm sure it's been a very long time since anyone did something nice for him." Michelle admired her work, then began snipping away as much of the beard as she could remove with the scissor. She shook the can of shaving cream. "Now the hard part. I've never shaved a man's face. I'll leave him a mustache for now."

After lathering the beard, she gingerly shaved him. A gaunt face emerged, miraculously, without cuts.

"Looks like those pictures of Lincoln," Sara said. "Before he grew a beard."

"He's at least that skinny. We'll take pictures, then let him rest while we make charts to keep track of his progress and e-mail the new pictures to Frank."

* * *

By the end of the day, Les decided that the man posed no threat to his grandchildren. Before he left, he reminded Michelle to lock her door. She assured him that she would, but doubted if she could even entice her guest into the house with food.

The next morning she held classes without an armed guard. Her guest sat on the steps outside of the classroom until she brought him a cushioned lawn chair.

"He has no fat for padding. He doesn't need to sit on concrete."

"If he won't come in," Keith said. "Where does he go to the bathroom?"

"I showed him the old outhouse, and I've seen him go in. I think we need to give him a name."

"Barney!"

"Not Barney. Let's just think about it for a while. Something will come to us. Get out your spelling books. This afternoon we'll go to the horse pasture for our science lesson."

* * *

Before he could follow them to the horse pasture, the kids had to reintroduce him to the dogs under better circumstances. He cowered near Michelle for some time. They encouraged him until he relaxed enough to play with both dogs.

She tried not to think about him while she compared horse to human anatomy, explained why horses and cattle could eat grass, and quizzed the kids on horse colors and markings. The discussion of grass led the kids to ask what he had eaten in the wilderness. Michelle began searching for edible plants.

"Michelle."

"Just a minute, Matt."

"Michelle."

"Wait."

"But, Michelle, he's on Coaly."

She forgot the root in her hand. Her guest sat on the rugged black, smiling. When Coaly moved off, she had visions of her fragile guest with multiple fractures. Coaly had bucked her off when she tried to ride with just a halter. Nothing controlled the gelding now. Coaly moved into a lope.

"Oh, no. God, let him come off someplace soft."

Coaly circled, executed a flying change of leads and finished a figure eight before continuing in a straight line. The rider somehow had control of the horse. She gasped when he slid to a stop, pivoted, and bolted in the other direction.

"Geez, he's a good rider," Matt said.

"Just imagine what he can do when he's in shape." He slowed Coaly and returned, smiling. But when he dismounted, his legs threatened to buckle. Michelle caught him. "You did too much. We'd better get you back to the house for a nap."

Les opened the gate for them.

"Those high-priced horse trainers don't put on a prettier demonstration. He's a horseman."

"A tired one."

"Frank called. He's on his way out. He hasn't found a matching missing person report from Wyoming. He's expanding the search. Was just going to add Utah and Colorado until I told him about the tan line. We forgot that yesterday. He'll send his description to Texas, New Mexico, and Arizona too. But he told me the fingerprints don't match any known criminal."

"I knew that."

"How could you know he's not a criminal?"

"His eyes. He has kind eyes."

Les rolled his.

"Guess if you're not afraid of him, it should say something." He parted company with them.

"I think we should call him Phillip. It means lover of horses."

"Sweet!" Matt said.

"It's perfect," Sara agreed. "The sheriff's here."

"Good. You kids take your recess while we draw his blood."

"Can we watch?"

"No. Go to the playground. We don't want to make the lab tech nervous."

V.

Michelle woke to the sound of distant thunder. Wind whistled past the house. *If it rains, he'll get soaked. I have to get him inside.* When she turned on the porch light, she found Phillip cowering on his mattress. He attached himself to her leg.

"Ah-h. This will be a whole lot easier if I can walk."

She pried his arms loose and dislodged him from the mattress to drag it into the house. Standing inside the door, she tried to coax him in. He resisted as a steady rain began. Occasional wind gusts dampened both of them.

"Come on, Phillip, we're going to get soaked."

Lightning flashed, followed almost immediately by thunder that shook the windows. He pushed past her into the house.

"That works too."

She sat beside him on the mattress and he snuggled up to her, whimpering. He jerked with every clap of thunder.

"You must have ridden out a lot of storms with no shelter, all by yourself this spring. Guess I'd be scared too."

She rocked until the thunder no longer affected him, then encouraged him to lie down. But when she stood to leave, he grabbed her hand. An instant of panic gripped her, before she pushed the bad memory away.

"Okay, I'll stay."

She lay behind him, stoking his hair until she fell asleep.

* * *

"No!"

The male voice jerked Michelle from a deep sleep.

"What do you want from me?" Phillip asked. "I'll tell you anything. Why don't you ask me something? No! No!"

She waited, hoping that he would say something to reveal his identity, but he began screaming in pain. She had to wake him. Maybe his ability to speak would continue when he woke. She shook him.

"Wake up. You're safe with me."

He snapped to a seated position, then melted into her arms sobbing.

"What's your name?"

No response. She wiped her own tears. His captors had tortured him simply to inflict pain. She could not comprehend such cruelty. Did they pick him in particular, or had he been a random victim? Had they victimized others? She wanted answers.

* * *

How much weight has he gained?" Bev asked.

"Twenty-five pounds," Michelle said, rinsing soap from Phillip's hair.

"He doesn't look like a refugee anymore."

"Yeah. It's not just the weight. His skin and hair are in better condition. He still looks thin, but healthy."

"I'm revising my estimate of his age."

"No kidding. I guess food is the fountain of youth."

"He's closer to thirty than fifty."

"And I'm beginning to think he won't be bad looking with another twenty-five pounds."

"I didn't think you'd notice things like that."

"Just because I don't want a man to touch me doesn't mean I'm blind."

"Has he?"

"Touched me? Not like a man. Like a scared kid. Do you think I'd keep him around if I had to fight him off?"

"Guess not. Have you figured out his tattoo?"

"There's still a scar over it. But I think it's a circle with flames inside."

Phillip reached for the hose and Michelle handed it to him. She shrieked when he turned it on her. He giggled and looked at Bev, who shook her finger.

"Don't you dare, young man!"

He obeyed and Michelle retrieved the hose.

"He has a sense of humor."

"I suppose that's good. Does he understand anything you say?"

"I think he still understands tone and body language better. Like just now when you scolded him. But I repeat things a lot. And he's beginning to recognize some words. He likes to be clean. When I say 'bath time,' he brings the hose. It's not much more than you'd expect of a trained animal. I thought he'd come around with kindness."

"He is coming around. You're just expecting too much. He's not afraid of the men anymore. He doesn't startle so easily. And if he recognizes some words, more will come."

"You're right. I'm just afraid they'll lock him up. If I could even get him to eat with silverware, he'd look more human to whoever comes for him."

"You're a teacher. You'll think of something."

Bev returned to the ranch house and Phillip climbed from the pool. After he dressed, Michelle handed him a comb. He had learned to comb his own hair after she demonstrated three times. Brushing his teeth had taken two lessons, although she had refined his technique over a few days. Shaving had taken three. He had removed the mustache as soon as he mastered the technique.

He seemed to learn everything after two or three lessons. Except eating with silverware. He devoured his three meals and five snacks as if she might snatch them away. She had begun fastening a towel around his neck to keep him clean.

"Today, you learn how to tie shoes."

He followed her to the porch. He pulled on socks, then an old pair of hiking boots. She sat beside him and demonstrated on her own boots. Frowning, he watched her tie a boot once, twice, three times. Then, he tied his own.

She hugged him.

"That's great, Phillip. Good job." He smiled. "You like praise. You like to hear, 'good job.' The more consistent I can be, the faster you'll learn."

* * *

The next day, the final day of school, Michelle filled a backpack for her class picnic. Today, she intended to make it to Cougar Rock. She let Phillip carry the pack, since he would eat most of the food. With the Winchester over her shoulder, she led the way across the creek, the kids chattering behind her. They covered more ground because she did not stop to teach. When she finally called a rest stop, she turned to find Phillip at the rear of the line.

She stared for a moment, not knowing how to react without him stepping on her heels. *Is he being responsible?*

"Matt, did Phillip decide to take up the rear?"

"Yeah. He just waited for me to go ahead. He usually follows you like a puppy."

"That's a good sign. He's acting like an adult."

After a few minutes, she forged ahead with a smile. She felt so good that she almost forgot the limitations of her smallest students. When she finally thought of another rest stop, she found Phillip carrying Tim.

"I'm sorry. We went a little far that time. We'll take a longer rest."

She called the next stop at the Stadium, thinking about how the last trip there had changed all their lives. Phillip might not have survived much longer. His physical condition had improved so much with proper nutrition. He even had the strength to carry a little boy on a strenuous climb.

They reached Cougar Rock in time for lunch. Michelle picked a spot where a few twisted trees and some boulders provided welcome shelter from the wind. She set her lunch aside and gave Phillip the rest. He gobbled everything before she finished, then eyed her fruit cup.

"Forget it. You'll survive until we get home."

His eyes followed the spoon from cup to mouth.

"Wait a minute. Maybe." She handed him the spoon, and offered him the fruit cup. When he tried to take it, she pushed his hand away. "Use the spoon."

She stopped him several times, then moved his hand with the spoon, to the fruit. Almost in slow motion, he scooped out fruit and put it in his mouth. Each succeeding spoonful came faster, until he finished the cup. She hugged him.

"Oh, Phillip, good job. I knew you could do it."

He smiled and took the cup from her, licking out the last of the juice.

"He did it," Sara said. "But he'd just as soon use his hands."

"We have to be happy with baby steps. He's learning to be a person again."

VI.

Terry stared as Michelle and Phillip rode up to the barn.

"That's Ginger, isn't it?"

She dismounted.

"Yes. I have no way of explaining to him that she's not broke."

Phillip slid off Ginger's bareback and the filly followed him into the barn where he brushed her coat.

"She didn't give him any problems."

"No. She was a little confused at first, but by the time I had Chief saddled, he had her turning whatever direction he wanted. He controls them by shifting his weight and touching their neck. We put on five miles."

"If he's around much longer, she'll be broke. Think you could get him to ride Fortune? He could use some work."

"He doesn't consult me when picking a horse."

"Well, he's good for our horses."

She finished unsaddling and strolled to the house, settling into a chair. Phillip lay on his bed with a sigh.

"You still don't have a lot of endurance. It's coming. You're not sleeping as much."

She heard a vehicle traveling the five-mile long driveway. This far out, they rarely had visitors. When Frank's SUV appeared,

Phillip sat up. Frank stopped by the ranch house, then hurried to catch up to the large man who emerged from the passenger seat and marched toward Michelle.

Phillip bolted around the corner of the house. She met the men at the same speed.

"Frank, you know better!"

"I tried to tell him, Michelle. I talked myself blue all the way out here."

"Detective Brady, Arizona State Police, miss. I need to see Captain Mc Kay." He tried to push past her, but Michelle kicked him in the shin. He howled. "Sheriff, you saw it. She assaulted an officer."

"You tripped. If you don't quit acting like a bull in a China shop, you won't accomplish anything."

"Look, miss. I've been on this case since Captain Mc Kay disappeared. This is the first break we've gotten. You're interfering with an officer in the performance of his duty."

"And you're acting like an idiot," Michelle said. "Phillip won't come near you if you don't back off."

"Phillip? Get out of my way."

He tried to shoulder her aside, then froze and stepped back. Michelle noticed his eyes, intimidated, focused over her shoulder. In slow motion, she turned, seeing the snarling, two-legged animal who had stopped the detective.

"Phillip, it's okay. He won't hurt me."

She attempted to push him back, but Phillip nudged her behind him. In the meantime, Frank had propelled a now-cooperative Brady toward the cruiser. For the first time, she noticed the other two men who had come with Frank. And the commotion had brought her father and brothers. Phillip, pacing the edge of her lawn, ignored everyone except Brady.

"You okay?" Les asked.

"Yeah. He's protecting me."

"So it seems. Quite a turn around."

"I know." She wiped her eyes. "They'll think he's insane and lock him up."

"We'll do our best to make sure that doesn't happen."

"Randy." All eyes turned to the dark-haired man in his thirties, who had approached the lawn. "Randy, it's me, Carlos. Good to see you."

Phillip glared at him for a moment, then turned his scowl on Brady again. Michelle rubbed his arm and addressed Carlos.

"That's his name? Randy Mc Kay?"

"Yeah. Captain Randy Mc Kay, state arson investigator. We all thought he'd been murdered." He pinched the bridge of his nose to control his emotions. "I never thought I'd see him alive again. He looks awful."

"To us, he looks great. He's gained more than 30 pounds."

"I saw the pictures. I didn't recognize him. After the first couple weeks, the search was for his body. Even before that, we didn't have much hope. Nobody expected to find him alive."

"Why would anyone do this to him?"

"Torture him? I don't know. We thought they'd killed him because he was investigating a high profile case involving organized crime. But I can't figure out what information they hoped to get from him."

"They didn't want information. Phillip can't communicate, but he talks when he has nightmares. He wants to know what they want, why they don't ask him anything. I think they tortured him just to inflict pain."

"Sadistic bastards. Why'd you call him Phillip?"

"We needed to call him something. It seemed appropriate because it means lover of horses."

For the first time, Carlos smiled.

"The Pied Piper of horses. They follow him. We knew right away this was a criminal investigation. They found Goldie grazing by his pickup in the national forest. If he'd fallen off, or even been killed, Goldie would've stayed with him."

Carlos had worked his way closer to the lawn without alarming Randy.

"Who's the other guy?"

"A state shrink."

She groaned.

"He'll think Phil ... Randy's a lunatic. They can't lock him up. He hates being cornered."

"I don't think his parents will let that happen."

"Carlos, I'm sorry, I don't know the rest of your name."

"Captain Carlos Paul, but Carlos is fine."

"Tell me about his parents."

"Nice people. His dad's in the newspaper business and has a big ranch in northern New Mexico. Randy was born with a silver spoon in his mouth, but you'd never guess it. He didn't have to work, but he wanted to help people. He gets that from his parents. They'll want to do what's best for him, even if that's unconventional."

"Oh, I hope you're right. He doesn't have a wife or girlfriend?"

"No. He broke up with his last girlfriend about a week before he disappeared. His mom has been after him for years to settle down and have kids. But every time he gets interested in one, she turns out to be a gold digger. I think that's been hardest on his parents. He's an only son."

"How long have you known him?"

"Five years. Since he started at the State Fire Marshall's office."

"How old is he?"

"His birthday was in April. He must be 29 now."

"At first, even after we cleaned him up, he looked closer to fifty. I know it's trivial, but what's his tattoo. He had a wound over it."

"No fires. You know, the circle and slash with flames inside."

"Oh. I won't grill you any more. But you can imagine, we've had a lot of questions."

"Yeah. You really care about him, all of you. Thank God you found him."

The psychiatrist approached, earning a brief glare from Randy. He had been too far away to hear their conversation.

"Miss Bowman, if I returned with an ambulance, would you slip Captain Mc Kay a sedative and ..."

"No!" That reply focused Randy's attention on the doctor. He snarled. "Oh-h. Why'd I have to do that?"

"You see, he's behaving like an animal. He's unpredictable."

"Heck," Frank said from his spot just off the lawn. "I'll predict his behavior. We get Brady out of here and he'll calm right down. What you think, Les?"

"Sounds 'bout right to me. I wasn't too sure of him at first. But I've seen enough to know that he takes care of those that treat him good."

The doctor scowled.

"He belongs in a hospital. His parents will be here tomorrow to get him the help he needs."

"Good," Michelle said. "Then the decision will be made by people who love him, not people who think they know what's best for him."

"You two head back to the car," Frank said. "I'll be along in a minute. If Brady hadn't acted like a bull in a China shop, he could have given you some useful information. Keep your guns handy and watch out for an old, tan Blazer with Utah plates. It was spotted in the national forest where he disappeared. They thought it was just a tourist until he showed up here."

"It's a hundred miles to the Utah border," Les commented. "How'd he get here."

"Who knows. If that Blazer shows up, arrest 'em all. Don't take any chances. Hog tie them and call me. These people are dangerous."

"Don't need to tell me twice."

* * *

Frank arrived with Elizabeth and Kendall Mc Kay at 10:30. His powers of persuasion had worked better on Randy's parents. They approached Michelle's house with care. Michelle hurried after Randy when he took up his guard post. She rubbed his arm, trying to lower his defenses.

"It's okay, Randy. This is your mom and dad. Do you remember them?"

Tears poured down Mrs. Mc Kay's cheeks and she held a ring-encrusted hand to her mouth.

"Randy, honey, it's Mom. We missed you so much, honey."

She held out the other hand, equally covered with rings, but Randy ignored her, glaring at his father. Her sobs distracted him. As she inched closer, his expression softened and he eventually wrapped an arm around her. She buried her face against his chest.

"Does he know her?" Mr. Mc Kay asked.

"I don't think so." Michelle said. "He probably just can't stand to see a woman cry."

"He's always been soft-hearted. The sheriff showed me what he looked like when you found him. You've done wonders. He says you'd like to continue to care for him."

"I'm a teacher. I have all summer off. We've seen what happens when he's cornered. We think that locking him in an institution would do more harm than good."

"What happens?"

"He panics. He tries to get away, even if that means harming himself."

"We won't have him locked up."

Randy's mother pulled away from her son a little.

"We'll take him home."

"Liz, how can we get him home?"

"Why, we'll just ..."

She began crying again.

"Mrs. Mc Kay," Michelle said. "I know you want him home, but it'll be a while before he's ready for that. I can help get him ready."

"Great idea. Isn't it, Liz? We'll do everything we can to support that effort. Have you found a way for a doctor to see Randy?"

"No. Frank brought a female lab tech out here to draw blood. We wanted to make sure he didn't have any infectious diseases. After seeing the results, our local doctor had us put him on a liquid vitamin and mineral supplement. You'd have to find a female doctor who's willing to make a major house call."

"We'll find one. When we do, she'll need those test results. She'll probably want to draw more blood to check his progress. Is that a problem?"

Michelle squirmed.

"I hate needles. But maybe this time, I won't have to play guinea pig for him."

"You have to demonstrate for him?"

"If it will hurt. Otherwise, he treats it as an attack."

"I see. We can't expect you to keep him for free. To put on so much weight, he must be eating you out of house and home."

"Well, as a matter of fact, we've never seen anyone eat so much. I wonder when he'll realize that there'll be more food later."

Les strolled over.

"Morning, Frank. Welcome, Mr. and Mrs. Mc Kay."

"Mr. Bowman. I'm Kendall. This is Liz."

"Les. You folks want to stick around a few days, see how your boy's doing?"

"We couldn't impose."

"Nonsense. We're fifty miles from town. If you want to spend time with him, the only thing to do is stay here. All our kids have moved out of the house. We have plenty of room."

"Well, thanks. Of course, we want to spend time with him. It will be difficult to pull ourselves away."

"It's settled, then. Frank can go back to town and we'll take you back when you're ready."

* * *

"We eat outside a lot," Michelle explained to her guests at suppertime. "He'll only come in the house during a thunderstorm." She dished up Randy's food. "If I let him help himself, he won't stop until he empties the bowl."

"He eats like he's still starving," Kendall said from the end of the picnic table, as close as Randy would tolerate him.

"I hope he'll get over that eventually." Randy picked up his steak, but she intercepted him before he could get it to his mouth. "No." She pushed his hands down. "No." He submitted, cutting off a large piece, then eating that with his hand. "Progress. Silverware is just too slow for him. He sees the advantage of a spoon with some foods, but why cut up meat when he can just bite it off?"

"You have a way with him," Liz said. "Does he understand you?"

"You've probably noticed I repeat myself a lot. He's beginning to recognize certain words by association. I know he's smart. It's almost like we speak a different language."

"If that was the problem, he'd communicate with sign language. He has the mind of a child."

"I would have agreed completely a couple weeks ago. But protecting me and some other behavior has seemed very mature. I'm not so sure anymore."

"One thing's certain. We need to tell Robin to move on with her life. She can't wait around for Randy. This could take a very long time."

"Robin?"

"His girlfriend," Kendall said. "She was devastated when he disappeared. She came out and spent a week with us in February. She was planning to move in with him. They were talking about marriage."

Michelle frowned, but withheld comment, instead refilling Randy's plate.

"The poor girl will find it hard to let go," Liz added. "But this isn't the Randy she knew." She bit her lip. "You will be yourself again, Randy. I know you will."

"Tell me about Randy."

"He was a wonderful child."

"He was a spoiled brat," Kendall said.

"We indulged him. We had two daughters during the first three years of our marriage, then Randy came along eleven years after Rachel. We were thrilled."

"He was pretty wild as a teenager, but about his senior year, he grew up. He spent that summer fighting wildfires, went to school for firefighting, then after another summer with the forest service, he got a job with the Scottsdale Fire Department. He kept taking classes and went to work for the state at 24. The youngest investigator ever."

"We were so relieved that he had a 'safer' job. Then this."

"Liz, we need to be grateful he's alive. We've been given back our son."

"Yes. That's a miracle."

"And, Michelle, your dad says that we owe it all to you."

"I don't know about that. My heart just went out to him. No one deserves what he's been through. I just had to help him."

"Thank you. We won't forget that. We'd like to send a psychologist to evaluate his condition. A female psychologist."

"Whatever you think is best. Just have her call ahead or she might end up waiting a few hours. We go for rides."

"Of course."

"Could you send some things to remind him of home. Not just to help him remember, but to make it more familiar when he does come home."

"Excellent idea. Should we send Goldie? We brought him home after Randy disappeared. He loves that horse."

"We have room for another horse." Michelle smiled. "My family might object because he's doing such a good job with our horses."

"Randy's trained every horse on our ranch. He can do things with horses the rest of us only dream of. I understand completely."

"We'll be happy to have Goldie here."

"And we can leave pictures with you," Liz said. "We brought a photo album."

VII.

Michelle touched her favorite picture. A smiling Randy with a twinkle in his eye, shirtless, muscles bulging as he lifted a nephew with each arm. She had correctly assessed his potential good looks. The words, "drop dead gorgeous" came to mind.

His breath, as he looked over her shoulder, created sensations that she had avoided for years. *I know why I'm feeling this. He's safe. If I'd met him when this picture was taken, I would've run.* But she could no longer pretend that her desire did not exist. Maybe spending time with him would remove her fear of other men.

"Now where was I? Oh. Mom. Dad. Susan. Rachel ..."

She pointed to each of his family members as she said the name. She had memorized brothers-in-law, nieces, and nephews. Liz would include pictures of the ranch staff with the package she had promised to send.

After the Mc Kays returned home, Bev had discovered a check for five thousand dollars in their room, "for Randy's board and ours."

Michelle smiled.

"So you were a spoiled, rich kid. I'd never have guessed."

He laughed and grabbed her around the waist. When she stiffened, concern replaced his smile. She rubbed his arms, trying to relax.

"It's okay. It's not your fault." She pressed her back against him. "Those sudden moves rattle my nerves."

He sighed and hugged her. Finally, her heart stopped pounding and the tension left her body. He felt hard. But instead of sharp angles, smooth muscles now covered his bones. A new sense of security engulfed her. Despite his inability to communicate, he had gained confidence. The roles of guardian and guarded had been reversed.

She turned with some effort and placed her arms around his neck. He grinned while she waited for a physical reaction. It came quite soon, but not from his body. She bit her lip.

"You have no idea what to do with a horny woman, do you." His expression remained. "Don't figure it out anytime soon, okay. If you start putting the moves on me, I'll go to pieces. Let's go for a swim."

He released her, recognizing the words. While Michelle changed, she questioned her motivation. *But I like to swim. I like it a lot more since Randy swims with me.* He saw no reason to wear clothes for swimming and seemed puzzled that she did. When he became playful, she enjoyed having him close to her.

"I feel like I'm taking advantage of a child."

She shook her head. *You told his mom he isn't a child. And you never do anything worse than hug him.* She shrugged, her conscience satisfied.

They hiked to the spot where a bend in the creek formed a pool. He stripped and jumped in while she laid a blanket on the grass. She floated in the pool, staying out of the current until he joined her.

"You make this too much like work. I swim to relax and cool off." She sat up and brushed the wet hair off his forehead. "Your mom said I could have someone out to cut your hair the way you used to wear it. I'll make some calls when we get back."

Michelle stopped talking when she caught him staring at her chest. He looked at his, then back at hers.

"Oh, great. You've noticed I'm shaped different." He rubbed his hand across his chest. "I see where this is going. Look, but don't touch." He stretched his hand. "No." Intent on his task, he caressed her. "No!"

Randy jerked back when she slapped his hand. His lip quivered and his eyes glistened.

"Oh-h. Don't do that. You know what 'no' means. You weren't ignoring me, you just had other things on your mind. I guess I got your attention. Give me your hand."

He tried to pull away, but she persuaded him. She kissed it.

"Better?" Again. "All better?" Again. "All better?"

A smile tugged at the corner of his mouth. When she kissed his hand again, he began giggling and splashed her.

"Hey!"

✳ ✳ ✳

Randy, still cautious around strangers, stood back while the haulers unloaded the palomino. Goldie winded him and neighed.

"After you get his shipping boots off," Michelle said. "Take off his halter too."

The haulers looked at each other, but complied. Goldie floated to Randy, who caressed the gelding's coat, then buried his face in the white mane. After a moment, he grabbed the mane and swung up on his horse.

His exhibitions on the ranch horses paled in comparison to what followed. Michelle had heard of, but never before seen, a horse and rider working as one. With no visible cues, Randy put Goldie through a series of gymnastics, even jumping a four-foot fence into a pasture and stopping to open and close the gate on the way out.

When he rode up to her, everyone in the yard applauded. Matt shouted.

"Sweet!"

"We thought he was good with our horses," Les said. "Amazing what he can do with one that knows him."

Randy dismounted and Goldie followed him to Michelle's house. He lay in the shade on the lawn while his horse grazed beside him. She watched them from the porch until Bev joined her.

"Guess the kids won't have to mow my lawn with Goldie here."

"He'll wreck it."

"That's okay. That horse is the first thing Randy's recognized. If he stomps on my flowers, it's worth it."

"I suppose. That haircut sure looks a lot better than the ones you were giving him."

"Amen!"

"A few more pounds and he won't be skinny."

"He's looking good, isn't he."

"Very handsome. Michelle, sooner or later, he'll start acting like a man."

Michelle bit her lip.

"He hasn't yet. Why worry about what might happen?"

"I don't want you to worry about it. I want you to have a plan."

"Randy understands the word no. He wouldn't hurt me. If I get upset, I can see he wonders what he's done to upset me."

"What *has* he done?"

"Nothing. Sometimes he makes a sudden move and I get unnerved."

"Oh. Is having him around helping with your fear?"

"Yes. If I can find a man sensitive to my past, I can even see marriage in my future."

Bev's eyes glistened and her lip quivered.

"Oh, Michelle. He's really been a blessing."

* * *

The sound of a car in the driveway distracted Michelle from rinsing Randy's hair. Peering over the top of the bushes, she saw a woman pull up in a maroon Subaru.

"Who could that be?" Randy rose, but when he saw the visitor, relaxed. Michelle handed him a towel. "You have to get dressed even if it is a woman."

"Michelle Bowman?" the woman said after emerging from her car.

"Yes."

"I'm Dr. Fontaine. The Mc Kays sent me to evaluate Randy's psychological state. May I come into your yard."

"You might want to wait until he gets dressed."

"Does he care?"

"No. He's not shy at all.

Dr. Fontaine rounded the bushes. She and Randy eyed each other while he finished drying.

"I saw pictures when you found him. His recovery is remarkable."

"Food is a miracle drug. You were supposed to call before you came."

"I wanted to come unannounced."

"Well, if you do that again, don't count on us being here. We go for long rides sometimes."

"Do you always bathe him?"

"I never bathe him. I wash his hair. He likes being clean. He brings the garden hose when he thinks it's time for a bath."

"He could wash his own hair too."

"I suppose."

"Then why do you do it?"

"Just a habit, I guess. I did it when we found him because he wasn't strong enough."

"If he doesn't need help, it's inappropriate for you to watch him bathe."

Michelle counted to ten under her breath.

"I know you have Randy's best interests at heart. Try to remember that I do too. I'm not trying to take advantage of him."

"I'm here because his parents think this is the best place for him. But a man who has been so badly traumatized should be hospitalized under the care of professionals. This situation is ripe for exploitation."

"Well, it won't happen. We cared about Randy before we knew his name. We still care about him." Randy finished pulling on his jeans and stepped toward Dr. Fontaine, between the two women. The doctor retreated. Michelle rubbed his arm. "It's okay, Randy. We're just having a little disagreement. Nothing for you to worry about. Smile, doctor. He doesn't like your attitude."

Dr. Fontaine forced a smile, then forced herself to relax. She spoke in a very friendly manner.

"You have him trained."

Michelle gritted her teeth, then managed to speak lightly.

"He knows who his friends are. He chooses to defend me. No one had to train him. He doesn't understand our words. Just our tone. You'll never accomplish anything if you keep attacking me."

Satisfied that Dr. Fontaine posed no threat, Randy finished dressing. She watched him.

"Very well. But understand, my duty is to Mr. Mc Kay. I will be watching for any sign that you are taking advantage of him. I won't hesitate to report my findings to his parents."

"Good. Because there'll be nothing to report."

VIII.

Michelle heard the door open and close at the same time she noticed lightning. Turning on the light, she found Randy huddled on his bed in the kitchen. She sat with him. When he lay his head in her lap, she stroked his hair.

"You come in yourself and you're not as afraid of the storms. You're getting better. It's just a matter of time."

She slept with her arms around him. But when she woke the next morning, she found their positions reversed. She lounged there, reluctant to disturb him. *Clomp.* She frowned. That sounded like a horse hoof on wood. *Clomp.* She glanced at the window in the door and giggled. Long, white hair. Goldie had taken Randy's spot on the porch.

"I'll bet he made a mess."

Several more hoof beats followed as Goldie walked off the porch. Then the door opened and Bev stepped in, already talking.

"Michelle, you had a horse on your porch. Where's Randy?" Bev stared and Randy jumped to his feet. "Michelle?"

"You're blocking the door, Mom. Let him out."

Bev stepped aside and he darted past her.

"Why were you sleeping with him?"

"Because he's afraid of storms. He comes in when it storms. He doesn't like to be alone."

"You're not locking your doors?"

"I haven't for a long time."

"Now I'll really worry."

"Mom ..."

"Let's put him to work. If we wear him out, I won't worry so much."

"What?"

"The reason I came over this morning. Your dad wondered if his parents would mind if he helped haul bales. You can never have too many strong men during haying season. He figured if we didn't ask his parents, it could be considered slave labor."

"Oh. His mom talked about that when she called Sunday. All of his lab work came back normal. She said if Randy were just visiting, he'd want to pitch in and help. So don't be afraid to put him to work. Kendall said it would be good for him."

"I've heard a saying something like, 'the best way to make a man is to think him so.' A man needs to work. Let's treat him like a man."

* * *

Michelle wondered if she would have trouble getting Randy to the hay field. But when she climbed into the pickup box, he followed. Chris and his wife rode in front, while Terry sat with Michelle and Randy.

"How do you plan to get him to load bales?"

"By example."

"He acts like a big, old dog."

"Don't call him that. He's a lot smarter than that."

"How smart can he be? He's loading bales when he doesn't have to."

Chris stopped by the first cluster of bales in the field and climbed out to let Emily drive. He and Terry began throwing hay on the long, low Donahue trailer. Michelle handed Randy a pair of gloves and pulled hers on. She picked up a bale and he copied her. They rode on the trailer between bunches. Terry stacked while the rest of them brought bales to him.

"You guys are killing me," he complained. "Michelle, why don't you come up and help me? They can handle that."

"Sorry. If I come up, so will Randy."

"Then take it easy. You don't have to work so hard."

She gladly slowed her pace, even taking her time getting off the trailer at each stop. When they had half a load, a hand held her down where she sat. She looked up at Randy's concerned eyes.

"You want me to rest?"

He left his hand on her shoulder a little longer before getting back to work. Chris shook his head.

"He's not dumb."

"That's what I keep telling people."

She climbed to the top of the load, catching a slight breeze. Across the creek, Les baled hay in another meadow. Hawks circled overhead and plummeted on mice exposed when the baler picked up the swath. She wondered if the rhythmic thumping of the baler or the sight of it attracted them to the easy meal.

A sweat-soaked, stinky T-shirt hit her in the face. Terry laughed.

"Throw that in the pickup for me."

Chris also shed his shirt. They all noticed Randy studying Michelle. She smiled.

"Don't look at me. You can take your shirt off if you want to."

"Aw, come on, Michelle," Chris said. "He depends on you. He won't do it if you don't."

"Very funny." She climbed down while they rode to the next bunch and pulled Randy's shirt off over his head. "There you go."

She patted his chest. He slapped her hand. Both of her brothers laughed.

"Why'd he do that?"

Michelle blushed.

"Because I slapped his hand when he touched my chest."

More laughter.

"Well, Randy," Terry said. "There's hope for you yet."

* * *

During Dr. Fontaine's next two weekly visits, she administered intelligence tests designed for infants and toddlers who had not developed verbal skills. With Michelle's encouragement, Randy sailed through both.

Dr. Fontaine spent the rest of her time observing and taking notes, rarely saying a word. Randy sometimes cast a puzzled glance at her. Michelle, for her part, felt as if the doctor waited for her to make a mistake. Her conscience had already convinced her not to enjoy his body quite so much. Although he still hugged and wrestled with her, she reacted more conservatively.

She shrieked when he snatched her off her feet and deposited her in the kiddy pool. He laughed.

"Randy!" She splashed him and he slid in with her, rolling around in the water. "Randy! Now stop that!" Despite her concern about Dr. Fontaine's reaction, she smiled. "I have to go change clothes."

He would not let her up. Finally, the doctor spoke.

"I see he really listens to you."

"If I got serious, he would."

"But you like his attention."

"He's a lot of fun."

"Are you having a sexual relationship with him?"

Michelle sputtered and her cheeks felt hot.

"Okay. I'll explain why that's such a stupid question. When I was nineteen, I was sexually assaulted. I haven't been able to let a man touch me since. Randy doesn't bother me because he acts like a kid. He doesn't know what sex is."

Michelle felt gratified to see Dr. Fontaine at a loss for words. Randy scowled, his mood subdued by their tone. Michelle patted his arm while the doctor cleared her throat.

"I see. I can't explain why he isn't sexually active. He's functioning at an animal level. Procreation is one of the most basic urges."

"I think he's functioning at a childlike level. That explains it for me. He's not an animal."

"That's very naive. He has an adult, male body. The urges will come. For your sake, I intend to recommend to his parents that he be given drugs to suppress those urges."

Michelle bit her lip.

"Whatever they think is best."

* * *

When Michelle next spoke to Randy's parents, Liz wasted no time giving her opinion.

"Oh, Michelle, do you know what that quack wants us to do?"

Kendall contradicted.

"Liz, we don't like it, but she's just thinking of Michelle's safety."

"I know what she wants, and I'm not concerned about my safety. I think she's overreacting. She tends to do that."

She could almost hear a collective sigh of relief. Liz's voice cracked when she spoke.

"Oh, thank, God. I couldn't stand to have Randy chemically castrated. How dare she even suggest it."

"It's a dumb idea. Randy understands the word 'no.' He wouldn't hurt me."

"We don't care for Dr. Fontaine," Kendall said. "But we didn't have a big selection of psychologists who were willing to see Randy at your ranch. Our doctor strongly advised that we have someone observe him. We can do better after he's home."

"What's she accomplishing?"

"Nothing. But—and we see no reason for this—other people think that someone needs to keep an eye on you. We know you're trustworthy."

"Thank you. But it's sensible."

"Could you handle a week long visit from us the end of the month?"

"I don't see why not. I'll clear it with Mom and Dad."

"When we come, we'll coordinate plans for Randy's future. The three of us need to work together to get him home."

* * *

When Michelle and Randy returned to the barn after a ride, they found Chris and Terry replacing a section of corral fence. Randy stopped to help. Michelle watched, noticing how her brothers had learned to communicate with him using hand signals. He retrieved materials and held rails while they pounded spikes.

She drifted toward the house, watching Randy. He kept working. She reached her lawn without him showing any sign of anxiety. *Great! He can get along without me.* She walked to the door. As she reached for it, Terry shouted.

"Michelle!"

She turned in time to see Randy racing after her. Her shoulders sagged.

"So much for that idea." He threw his arms around her, shaking. She hugged him. "I was just going in the house. I go there all the time when you're on the porch. I'm not leaving you."

"Bring a chair! We need the help!"

When Randy stopped trembling, she collected a water jug, one of his Tony Hillerman novels, and a chair before returning to the corral. He carried the chair for her. She selected a shady spot beside the barn and opened the book. After a few anxious moments, he worked again. Terry commented.

"Sometimes he seems almost normal. Then he does something like that. Those bastards should get the same treatment they gave him and more."

"Amen," Chris agreed.

"He's come a long way," Michelle said. "I'm just not sure why he needs me for a security blanket. He's perfectly comfortable with the whole family. He acts like you guys when I'm around. Why's he fall apart when I leave him?"

"He either thinks you're his mother or his wife."

"Maybe his mom. Definitely not his wife. He doesn't have a clue about that kind of relationship."

"Still thinking like a kid. Randy, you got to grow up."

Randy grinned and Michelle's brothers laughed.

"Don't read anything into that," she said. "He just recognized his name."

IX.

Michelle led her horse from the barn and checked the cinch one last time. Randy swung up on Goldie as usual with no tack. She no longer felt amazed by the control he had over his horse. When they dismounted during a ride, Goldie grazed nearby. If he wandered too far, Randy simply walked away. Goldie hurried to catch him.

"Where should we ride today?" Randy watched her mount. "No opinion? Let's go up the valley and check cows."

He followed her on narrow trails and rode alongside when the terrain permitted. They saw dozens of Hereford cows grazing or laying down, chewing their cud. No sign of problems.

Aspen leaves rustled in the breeze near the creek. The pine and spruce trees freshened the air with their ever-present scent.

She rode uphill, out of the trees to a grassy slope. It would provide a good view of most of the open pasture in the valley. The slope ended in a massive rock wall. Over the centuries boulders, some as big as a van, had fallen, scattering near the top of the slope. She threaded her way through these, knowing where to find the best view.

A cougar snarled from one of the largest boulders. Michelle's gelding reared. She leaned forward and grabbed his mane to stay mounted. When he began coming down, she gathered the reins to control him.

Futile. The gelding bolted in a blind panic, charging down the slope toward home. She hauled on the reins without effect. Trying to pull him in a circle at this speed, on this slope, would only result in a wreck. He hurled her toward the trees with branches which would knock her off.

Her horsemanship training flashed through her mind. Emergency dismount. *Grab the mane. Swing your leg over. Land facing backward. You're less likely to get hurt.* She had to act before he reached the trees.

Michelle threw herself off the horse.

The slope interfered with the effectiveness of her dismount. She hit hard, then flipped heals over head and landed face down.

For a moment, nothing registered. Darkness and flashes of light competed for space in her brain. *I can't breath!* Her head began to clear. *I just had the wind knocked out of me. Give it a minute. Air will come.* She took a wheezing breath.

She raised her head, seeing hooves and white legs. *Don't run over me, Goldie.* Randy's feet dropped to the ground, then he kneeled beside her. She wheezed again. He caressed her back.

She looked past him at the white legs. This made no sense. *Why isn't Goldie running from the cougar? Yes, Chief overreacted. But Goldie shouldn't just stand there with a cougar so close. Maybe I'm hallucinating.*

Her breath began to come easier. She pushed herself up on her elbows, groaning. Randy's hands held her in place. He began probing, first her spine, then arms and legs. Though she winced a few times, his exam convinced her that she had no broken bones.

He helped her sit up and resumed caressing. Michelle looked around. Goldie stood nearly on top of them, his eyes trained up the slope.

"Does he trust you that much? You're not afraid, so he isn't.

That's amazing." Randy nuzzled her. "We have to get home. When Chief comes in without me, everyone will freak."

She tried to rise, producing a massive groan. He picked her up. "Home. We have to go home."

With great care, he lifted her to Goldie's back. She gripped the white mane and closed her eyes as the world began spinning. When she opened them, he watched her, looking concerned.

"I'm fine. Let's go home."

He swung up behind her, wrapping both arms around her waist. Goldie moved off at a fast walk. The motion made her stomach roll. She closed her eyes and leaned against Randy. For the next few minutes, awareness only consisted of her aching body, the scent of evergreens, and the safety of his arms.

* * *

"Michelle!"

Terry's voice roused her. She opened her eyes.

"I took a tumble."

"Randy, bring her up to the house."

"I don't have any broken bones. He checked."

"I think a doctor should be the judge of that."

"I can't go to a doctor! What would Randy do?"

"Don't be stupid. If anybody else got thrown from a horse, you'd have a fit if we didn't go in for x-rays."

Tears came to her eyes as her parents joined Terry.

"But what will Randy do? I can't leave him. Mom, I can't leave him."

"Then, he'll have to come along. At least as far as the hospital. It's a nice day. We can take you in the back of the pickup. Terry, get another mattress from the motor home. Michelle, are you comfortable there?"

"As comfortable as I can be. I hurt all over. But Randy checked for broken bones before he picked me up. He was great. Chief spooked at a cougar. He ran away. There's no excuse for that. I had to bail out before he took me through the trees."

"Did you hit your head?"

"Yeah. And knocked the wind out of me. Randy was right there. Goldie didn't spook at all."

"That's good. Come on, Randy. Bring her over to the pickup." She motioned and Goldie followed her. "Emily, get Michelle's kit."

Randy stepped off on the open tailgate. He, Les, Chris, and Terry eased Michelle to the mattress. Bev gave more orders.

"Pillows and blankets. I'll check her vitals before we leave. Les, are you driving?"

"You bet I am."

"I'll ride in back with Michelle. Someone needs to call the hospital. Tell them about Randy. We need to see only women outside the emergency room." Emily brought the first aid kit and Bev spent a few minutes examining Michelle. "Tell them her pupils are equal and react to light. Her blood pressure is on the low side. Put some of those pillows under her legs. Then let's go."

* * *

Michelle worried about Randy during the entire trip. He sat over her looking concerned.

"Mom, do you think he'll understand that I need to go inside?"

"He knows you're hurt, honey. As much as I'd like to be with you, I'll stay with him. I think he'll need me more."

"Thanks, Mom. Next to me, he trusts you most. How fast is Dad driving?"

"Fast. I'm trying not to look at the speedometer."

Michelle smiled.

"Glad I can't see it either."

"We're almost there."

Les slowed when he approached the outskirts of town. He eased to a halt near the emergency room door. The resident nurse practitioner met them, holding only a glass of water.

"Is she still stable?"

"Yes. Conscious and stable."

"Good." She reached in her pocket. "This is for Randy. Do you think you can get him to take it?"

"I'll try. Who came up with this idea?"

"Your son, actually."

Randy frowned and resisted for some time. After he swallowed the pill, he made an impatient motion toward Michelle. Bev patted his arm.

"Yes. Now we can treat her."

Les helped the nurse practitioner into the pickup and two nurses brought a gurney. Randy, Bev, and Les assisted with the transfer. Randy walked beside the cart until it neared the hospital door.

He held back, then fidgeted when they pushed Michelle inside. Anxiety registered as deep lines on his face. He began pacing outside the door.

Bev tried to sooth him without success. He pointed at the glass doors.

"Yes. Michelle's in there. They're taking care of her."

He pointed again.

"I'm sorry, Randy. I can't help you. I don't know what you want. I can't bring her out. Les is in there with her. She'll be fine. I hope whatever they gave you starts working soon."

Randy kept pacing, stopping only to point at the door again. Frank's SUV pulled into the lot. He joined Bev.

"The hospital called me as a precaution. How's Michelle?"

"I don't think she has a head injury. All of her limbs are working. She'll probably be fine. I don't know about him though. If any men approach, head them off."

"We'll do."

"They gave him something before they took Michelle in. I don't see that it's working."

"How long has it been?"

"Seems like an eternity. But it's probably only been ten minutes."

"Pill or shot?"

"Pill."

"Give it time."

Randy pointed at the glass again. This time, when Bev did nothing, he got behind her and nudged her toward the door.

"You want me to go inside?"

"Go ahead. I'll stay with him."

"I'll try it. See how he reacts." Bev opened the door and stepped inside, not letting it close. Randy's face showed relief. "Okay. I'll come back as soon as I know anything."

She found Les outside the x-ray department. His eyes widened. "That pill must really be something."

"No. Frank's with him. Randy insisted that I come inside."

"How could he do that?"

"He pointed, then shoved me toward the door."

"Huh. The doc's looking at her skull x-rays while they take pictures of her whole spine. Thank God Randy was with her. It would have taken hours for us to find her."

"Amen. I think she'll be fine. Just really sore for a few days."

"Hope so."

* * *

When Bev reached the parking lot, she found Randy sitting on the tailgate of the pickup, his head nodding, and Frank standing nearby. Randy raised his head.

"How is she?" Frank asked.

"Head and spine okay. They started an IV to combat shock. We're waiting on test results to tell if there are any internal injuries. And they took her back to x-ray. Looks like she has a broken little finger on her left hand."

"Great. I mean, not great that she has a broken finger, but great if that's all she has."

"Amen. I guess the drug's working."

"You should have seen me trying to get him up there. Like handling a drunk. Before you go back in, want to help me get him on the mattress? I'm afraid he'll fall off."

Bev complied, then found Michelle in the emergency room again, a splint on her finger. Les occupied a chair nearby. Michelle leaned forward, her brow furrowed.

"How's Randy?"

"Just about asleep."

Michelle lay back on the bed.

"Thank God. Now I just have to get out of here before he wakes."

"You'll do whatever the doctor tells you to, young lady."

"I'll stay if there's a good medical reason. But not just 'for observation.' You can observe me at home. It made sense to get checked out. But I can heal at home in my own bed."

"Okay. If there's no good medical reason. But we'll let the doctor make that decision."

They only waited a few minutes. The doctor informed them that Michelle could go home when the IV bag emptied, if she could stand without losing consciousness.

She accomplished that and slept beside Randy on the trip back to the ranch. Bev stayed on Michelle's couch that night. When Michelle woke, she found Randy sleeping on the floor beside her bed. She groaned as she tried to sit up. He roused and hurried to help her. Supporting her shoulders, he eased her to a sitting position.

"Bless you."

After Bev served them breakfast, she decided that she could go home. Randy seemed to intend to care for Michelle. However, she returned in little more than an hour. After small talk, she chewed her lip.

"You're comfortable having him in the house with you?"

"Yeah. Mom, you have to start trusting him. Hasn't he earned it?"

"Almost. He's still a man, Michelle. He has all the equipment and he's healthy. He could start functioning at any time."

"I'd have to show him how."

"Excuse me?"

"Mom, I had to show him how to brush his teeth, eat with silverware, tie his shoes, stack hay bales. The only thing he's done without teaching is ride and wash himself. I don't think sex will be an issue unless I'm stupid enough to show him how."

Bev scowled.

"I suppose. You could be right."

"Try not to worry so much."

* * *

That night, Randy made his bed beside Michelle's again. She unbuttoned the shirt she had worn all day. Her usual T-shirts had proven too painful and a bra was out of the question. He watched while she managed to remove the shirt without exposing her breasts.

"I need you to do something for me."

She squeezed analgesic on his hand before easing herself face down on the bed. He gazed at the cream on his hand. She motioned for him to come closer, then, painfully, guided his hand to her back. He began rubbing.

"Thank God. I don't think I had the energy to show you three times."

He massaged from shoulders to waist, so effectively that she woke later in the dark with the blankets pulled over her. *I'd better put a shirt on or Mom will freak in the morning.*

Randy turned on the light as soon as she stirred and helped her with the shirt.

The pattern repeated itself for the next week. When she could move without groaning and wear her normal clothes, he returned to the porch. Bev noticed.

"I've been waiting for that."

"I'll bet you looked out your window first thing every morning."

"You bet I did."

"I guess he stayed as long as he thought I needed him, but he still doesn't like feeling confined."

"Good. I'll worry less without him in your bedroom."

"Likely story. You'd only worry less if I kept my doors locked at night."

Bev smiled.

"Guilty. But you're right. He's earning my trust."

"I'm beginning to think that Randy's my guardian angel."

X.

Michelle opened her eyes, wide awake from a deep sleep. *But why?* The curtains rustled in a faint breeze. Crickets chirped. The glow from a yard light barely illuminated her room.

There! The hissing sound that had awakened her. One of Randy's angry sounds. He made it by blowing through his teeth.

Again. Then his growl, followed immediately by a whisper.

"What the ..."

Chaos erupted on her porch.

Michelle leaped from her bed and hit the panic button. Lights came on all over the ranch yard, flooding her bedroom like sunrise. She ran to the window.

Randy had a man on the ground in front of her house. She froze for a moment, shocked by the savagery of Randy's attack. A door slammed across the yard in the duplex, jarring her into action. She raced through the house and outside.

"Randy!"

He ignored her, beating the intruder with both fists. The man still struggled, but now without affect. Blood flew with each blow.

"Randy! No!"

He would kill the intruder unless someone stopped him. But

she could not bring herself any closer. She looked up, desperate, and saw her brother coming at a dead run.

"Chris, stop him!"

Chris seized Randy's upraised arm with both hands and heaved him off the man. He released the arm and sprang back as Randy lunged toward him. Randy took a swing, which Chris avoided. Terry arrived to back up his brother.

"Randy, easy now. Come on. You know us."

Randy glared at them, his chest heaving. His shoulders sagged and his fists unclenched. He whirled to face the intruder, groaning and coughing on the ground. Everyone held their breath until he stepped over the man and wrapped his arms around Michelle.

She broke down, sobbing so hard that she barely heard her father.

"What the blazes is going on?"

Chris explained.

"This guy must have tried to break into Michelle's house. Biggest mistake of his life."

"Who the heck is he? There ain't enough left of his face to tell. Terry, turn him on his side. He's choking on his own blood. Chris, go inside and call Frank."

Chris walked past Michelle and Randy to use the phone. The silence that followed caught her attention. She met Terry's gaze as he kneeled beside the intruder, holding his wallet. She took a deep breath.

"It's him, isn't it."

Terry nodded.

"Bob Wright. He's going back to jail. He violated his parole coming anywhere near you."

She shuddered and Randy stroked her hair. Bev arrived.

"What happened? Who is that?"

"It's the guy who assaulted Michelle," Les said. "Randy took care of him. Go tell the girls that everything's under control. I'm sure they're worried about the kids."

"Michelle, are you okay?"

"I will be."

Bev departed and Chris came from the house.

"Sheriff and ambulance on their way. Randy's bleeding all over you."

Michelle pulled back. A gash crossed his right forearm.

"Get my kit!" She guided Randy to a chair, but he refused to sit. "It's easier if you sit, but I guess I can treat you standing."

"Too much adrenaline," Les said. "He won't sit for a while."

Chris brought the first aid kit and unlatched it. She opened sterile gauze and pressed it to the four inch long cut.

"Open another package for me. The guy must have had a knife."

"Yeah," Terry said. "It's here next to your porch."

She took the gauze from Chris with a shaking hand.

"You sure you're okay, Michelle?"

She nodded.

"For now. I have to take care of Randy. If he hadn't been here ..."

"But he was. Maybe that's why God brought him here. To protect you."

She looked up at her brother and forced a smile.

"Yeah. Thank God. Get me another one. It's soaking through. Randy's knuckles are a mess."

"So's that guy's face."

"Terry, how's he doing?"

"Better than he deserves. He's breathing okay now. I'm sure he's got a broken nose and I'll bet he has a broken jaw. He's not really conscious. That guy, Brady, doesn't know how lucky he is."

"Yeah. Is there anything we can do for him before the paramedics arrive?"

"Maybe stop the nosebleed. Keep him on his side."

"Put some gloves on. Use some gauze to try to stop the flow. Don't apply any more pressure than you have to."

Bev returned.

"The kids didn't wake up. What can I do?"

"We need to clean up Randy."

"Will do."

"Chris, now tape. I've stopped the bleeding."

"Right. Why aren't *you* wearing gloves?"

"We've already tested Randy. I won't catch anything from him. We don't know about Wright."

"But a lot of this blood is his."

"I know. I hope he doesn't have anything that Randy could catch." Bev brought a towel and wash cloth. "I suppose you should cover that piece of trash with a blanket. We don't want him going into shock. And take his vitals. Show the paramedics that we made some effort."

Bev snorted.

"More than he deserves."

* * *

In the hour it took for help to arrive, Randy relaxed enough to sit in a chair, but kept his eyes on Wright. Michelle removed his bloody shirt and gave him a clean one. Bev brought her a robe because she would not leave his side. Les, Chris, Terry, and Bev by turns left to change clothes.

A deputy and ambulance pulled into the yard without lights or sirens. In this remote location, they had no traffic to warn.

Randy leaped to his feet. Michelle soothed him, while Les advised the paramedics how to proceed. The female paramedic took the lead, beginning Wright's treatment.

Randy ignored her, instead watching her male partner ease his way across the lawn. When Randy hissed, everyone paid attention. The man froze.

Michelle took Randy's hand and tried to move off. She would have had better luck trying to uproot a tree. Finally, he glanced at her, then began backing away. He put some distance between them and the house before pulling her into the shadows.

"You're shaking. I'm sorry, Randy. I should have gotten you out of there sooner."

"He wanted to watch Wright," Bev said beside them. "This night has been too much for him. He's exhausted, but he won't be able to relax until they're all gone."

Michelle squeezed him.

"We need to get that doctor out to look at him. If he cut his knuckles on Wright's teeth, he could get a bad infection. The human mouth is filthy. She gave him a tetanus shot when she was here before. So at least that shouldn't be a problem."

"We'll call her in the morning. And his parents. They need to know about this."

"Mom, could this come back to haunt Randy. I mean, they say you can only shoot an intruder if he's in your house. Wright only made it to my porch."

"No. Judges see things a little different out here. Just coming into the ranch yard is trespass enough. At night. With a knife. Violating his parole. No judge will fault Randy for defending you."

"Randy would have killed him if Chris hadn't stopped him."

"And I wouldn't have blamed him. But I'm glad he didn't. A judge couldn't have ignored that."

"Did the deputy collect that knife?"

"Yeah. He managed to do that without messing up. Frank should be here any minute. That deputy's so green, he's never seen anything like this. He called for backup."

"Good. Frank knows Randy. I feel better with him in charge."

* * *

When Michelle explained the situation to Randy's doctor, she agreed to clear her afternoon to see him. She would not arrive until late in the day.

To Michelle's relief, Kendall picked up the phone when she called. After assuring him that both she and Randy were in no danger, he took the rest of her report with more composure than she could have expected from Liz.

He asked for another call after the doctor saw Randy, then decided on an additional precaution. He would place a Wyoming lawyer on retainer in case the need arose.

Michelle sat beside Randy to keep him still while Dr. Combs administered IV antibiotics. For a little while, the hanging bag intrigued him. Then he watched the doctor examining his cut. She frowned.

"This should have had a few stitches. But I understand you did the best you could under the circumstances. If the scar really bothers him, he can have cosmetic surgery."

"It's not his only scar. Last night, I was afraid I wouldn't be able to stop the bleeding. I don't know what we would've done if the guy had stabbed him."

The doctor bit her lip, then applied fresh dressings to the wound.

"That's a very good point. Especially after your experience in the ER. I'll leave you a sedative, to be used only if Randy is badly injured. You're almost as well equipped as an ambulance service. What's your protocol if someone needs to be hospitalized?"

"Just what we did when I got thrown. We stabilize any injuries and transport them. Waiting for the ambulance wastes an hour. If we ever have a serious injury, we'll call the ambulance to meet us at the highway."

"So you're looking at an hour to the hospital. If you need to take Randy, give it to him just before you transport. I'll get permission from his parents to talk to emergency room personnel. They need to be prepared. If they don't keep him sedated, the results will be disastrous."

Michelle shuddered.

"I don't even want to think about it." Randy stroked her hair. "You really are my guardian angel."

"I see a change in him. Other than the obvious physical improvement. I think you're not far off. He believes that his purpose in life is to protect you."

"Oh. Is that good or bad?"

"Everyone needs a purpose. The first time I saw him, he still seemed lost. I think he was starting to find himself. Having a purpose gives him confidence. It's very good for him. Unfortunately, until he can regain his former identity, you're stuck with him. Separation would be devastating for him. He might never recover."

"Oh. His parents want him home."

"I'll talk to them."

XI.

Kendall and Liz arrived at the ranch in a Hummer. Michelle laughed.

"You didn't take any chances on our winding mountain roads."

"After the last trip," Kendall said. "I thought overkill was appropriate. Randy, good to see you, son."

Randy hugged both of his parents, reducing Liz to tears.

"That's so much better than last time."

"I go through the family pictures with him every day," Michelle said. "But he usually scowls when I say Susan's name."

Kendall laughed and patted Randy's back.

"You're in there, son. No doubt about that. I don't think he and Susan have ever gotten along. They just don't like each other."

"Susan and Randy both have strong personalities," Liz said.

"I'm not as generous as Liz. Susan has an abrasive personality. She and I barely get along. She used to work for me, but she quit in a huff."

"You're such nice people. How'd that happen?"

"Thanks. She's just spoiled rotten like the rest of our kids."

"Randy doesn't act spoiled. We don't need to stand here all day. Let's sit on the porch."

"What happened to your lawn?"

"Goldie. He's around the back of the house now. I make Randy clean up after him."

"Good for you. How's Randy healing?"

"Good. No sign of infection. Dr. Combs had me giving him shots. I had some training. And I've given shots to horses. But I was pretty shaky. Fortunately, he's very patient with me. Either that, or he has a high pain threshold."

"She tells us that we can't take him away from you."

"That's what she told me. I'm sorry."

"Nonsense. You saved his life. It's natural that he became attached to you."

Kendall and Liz exchanged glances. "We'd like to offer you a job caring for him."

"I'm already taking care of him."

"At our place. He can't come home without you. We can't expect you to come along for free. We'd like to hire you."

"But I already have a job. I've signed a teaching contract for the year."

"We considered that. We'll find someone to teach for you."

"Ah-h. Clear out here?"

"It's the kind of obstacle that can be overcome with money. Randy needs you and we want him home."

"I never wanted to live anywhere else. I came back here as soon as I finished college."

"We'll only ask you to commit for a year. That should be long enough at the rate Randy's improving. We'll pay you well. Free room and board. You'd stay in the guest house. It even has a porch for Randy."

"Um. I'll think about it."

"Good. While you're considering it, we'd like you to take Randy to town, stop at the airport. Make that part of his routine. When the time comes for the trip home, it'll be less traumatic."

"He'll go nuts if you lock him in a plane."

"Agreed. We'll have to sedate him. He'll wake up at home

with you by his side. He may feel disoriented, but he can handle it with you anchoring him."

Michelle nodded.

"Frank told me that Wright's lawyer wanted Randy locked up."

"Don't worry about it. The judge met with his attorney, your sheriff, and our attorney. Your sheriff really came through. He gave firsthand accounts of how easy Randy is to get along with if you pose no threat. Wright's attorney contended that he didn't deserve to have his jaw broken for violating his parole. The judge told him that Wright should thank Randy. He kept him from committing a more serious crime."

Michelle began trembling and Randy hugged her.

"Thank God he was here."

* * *

The next day, Liz joined Michelle and Randy for a swim. He now wore cutoff jeans for the activity, after observing Chris and Terry at the swimming hole. Michelle worried what Liz would think of some of her interactions with Randy, but tried not to change her routine. After her swim, she lay face down on the blanket and he sat beside her, rubbing her bare back.

"That looks very sensual," Liz said.

Michelle raised her head, blushing.

"It feels good, but it's completely innocent. He just knows I like it. I wouldn't take advantage of him."

"Oh, I know that. What would you do if he made a pass at you?"

Michelle stiffened and Randy began using both hands in the same gentle way. She sighed.

"I'd tell him 'no.' He understands that."

"Why?"

"Why?"

"I'd like to know why you'd refuse his advances."

"It's the ethical thing to do. I'd feel like I was taking advantage of him. And, besides, I'm just not ready for that."

Liz watched Randy for a moment.

"Do what's right for you. But if he should show interest in you as a woman, don't refuse him for ethical reasons. We want Randy to regain everything he had. Consider him a consenting adult."

Michelle stared.

"But he acts like a child."

"He's not acting like a child now. He wasn't acting like a child when he defended you from that intruder. Or took care of you after you fell. I'm not asking you to seduce him. If he shows interest, that will be adult behavior. I've listened to you. He only rarely acts like a child, doesn't he?"

"Well, I guess so. I thought if he acts that way sometimes, he thinks that way all the time."

"Maybe he sometimes has flashbacks and needs comfort."

"Flashbacks?"

"When those men tortured him for weeks on end ... he must have felt so alone. Maybe he feels that loneliness when you try to leave him. Maybe the storms remind him of being alone in the mountains."

"I suppose. Those are the only times he really acts like a kid. But if he thinks like an adult, why doesn't he have a sex drive?"

"I wish I knew. Those animals took so much from him. I want Randy back."

"I guess I don't really know Randy."

"Only parts of him. I see his sense of humor and his compassion. But he was a leader, a very passionate man. He always questioned. Now he follows blindly."

"Did he have a lot of girlfriends?"

Liz smiled.

"When he was younger. But in recent years, he's been searching for a wife. He's had steady relationships. I'd start getting hopeful and he'd break up with her. His usual reason, 'Just another gold digger.' He attracted them like flies."

"His friend said he didn't have to work."

"No. He has a trust fund. But we expected our children to work. We would rather have had him take a position at one of our papers. But Randy wanted to prove himself outside the family business. And he did. He was a very good firefighter and investigator."

"His friend called him brilliant."

"Someone said he had three things that make a good arson investigator: intelligence, keen powers of observation, and a suspicious nature."

"Bet that helped him weed out the gold diggers too."

Liz laughed.

"Yes. I hadn't thought of that."

* * *

Randy watched Michelle throw his mattress into the bed of the pickup, then followed her in. Bev paused before taking the wheel.

"Hope it doesn't rain."

"There's not a cloud in the sky," Michelle said. "I would've waited until next week if there were any rain in the forecast. Just remember to park away from the stores. The less people he has to deal with, the better."

"You've told me a dozen times. Let's go, Emily."

Michelle and Randy sat up, enjoying the view on the winding gravel road that led to the ranch. When Bev turned west on the pavement, Michelle lay down and he snuggled in behind her. In his arms, she felt like no one could hurt her.

I have to take that job. I can't lose him. That's insane! You can't be falling in love with a man you don't even know. This isn't the real Randy. That man won't follow you like a loyal dog.

She sighed. She had to give herself the chance to know the real Randy.

"I guess we're going to New Mexico." He raised his head, breathing in her ear. When she writhed, he smiled. "If you ever figure out what to do with your body, you'll be able to talk me into anything. You already know how to turn me on."

They lay together until the pickup neared the outskirts of town. Bev pulled into the airport and they watched spray planes take off and land for a few minutes. Michelle offered Randy something to drink, the planned method of giving him a sedative.

At the Wal-mart, Bev parked far from the door, well away from other vehicles. No one came near the pickup, but Randy stood, watching everything. Michelle rubbed his forearm until he sat on the edge of the box. When Bev and Emily returned with two laden shopping carts, he vaulted to the asphalt to help them unload.

"His parents raised him right," Bev said. "How'd he do?"

"Good. The grocery store will be the real test."

Before that, they picked up parts at the implement dealership. Its quiet lot did not bother Randy. Michelle's theory on the grocery store proved true. Bev could not park far enough from the activity for Randy's comfort. He stood the whole time she and Emily shopped. Michelle physically restrained him when a man walked too near the pickup. She let her breath out as her mother approached.

"Boy, I'm glad to see you. I hoped you wouldn't get your groceries at the drive up."

"I have more sense than that. He's not helping this time."

"He's acting as look out."

"Do you think he can handle the Burger King drive up?"

"It shouldn't be busy this time of day."

"What will he want?"

"Same thing I eat, just king size."

Liz ordered their lunch, then drove to a nearby park, where they ate in the shade. Michelle made her announcement.

"I'm taking the Mc Kay's job offer."

"Good." Bev sipped her drink. "Don't look so surprised. You can't stay here forever. I don't think we'll have any more grandkids at the ranch."

"Over my dead body," Emily said.

"In seven years you'll run out of students. You need to get out in the real world before you're forced to. You can come back in a year, if you want to."

"Of course I'll want to."

"Don't be so sure. You might like it where there isn't so much snow."

"Less snow. Oh-h. Does it snow in New Mexico?"

"In part of it. I don't even know where they live."

"They said the closest town we'd have heard of is Taos. I'll have to look at a map. I don't know where that is."

"I guess you should know where you're going. How soon will he be ready?"

"Well," Michelle ate fries. "A couple more trips to town should do it. Probably a month. When I put a timetable on it, reality sets in. I'm leaving the ranch. Wow."

XII.

Michelle stood on the porch, gazing at her parents' house.

"I suppose we can't put it off any longer without being rude," she said to Randy. "Hope you can handle all the new people."

Her brother and sister, with their families, had arrived for this annual gathering. She approached the deck, where all the men had congregated. Her brother-in-law, Pete, greeted her in his usual manner.

"There's trouble!"

"Sit down, Pete." Les said. "If you wrestle with her like you usually do, Randy'll be on you like stink on a billy goat. Tone it down."

"What's he, jealous?"

Michelle stopped on the edge of the deck and Randy stayed one step down, eyeing Pete. She responded.

"Protective. It takes him a while to warm up to strangers. If you're pushy, he'll keep his defenses up. If you wrestle with me, he'll beat you senseless."

"I'm not pushy."

"No," Terry said. "You're loud and obnoxious. Be on your best behavior."

"He has to do better than that," Chris added.

"Yeah. Try to act like a normal person. We taught him to play softball and we want him on our team tomorrow. He can't do that if he's watching you."

"Nobody's ever complained about me before," Pete said.

"We're used to you."

"Can I get a beer, or will that bother him?"

"Slowly," Michelle said.

Randy's eyes followed Pete as he moseyed to the cooler and back to his seat.

"He's never seen Roger either. Why isn't he watching him?"

"I'm not loud and obnoxious."

Michelle smiled.

"Well, that may have something to do with it. But Roger looks like Terry and Chris. Randy can see that he's a relative."

"Let's see." Roger brought her a chair, earning a long glare from Randy. "What would he have done if Pete had tried that?"

"You know what happened to the guy who tried to break into my house. I don't think his reaction would be that extreme. But it's best not to push him." Randy sat on the deck railing beside Michelle, still watching Pete. "He's coming around."

"How long will this take?" Pete said. "I'm tired of sitting here like a bump on a log."

"Everything with Randy takes patience."

"Michelle," her sister called from inside the kitchen. "What're you doing out there with all those Neanderthals?"

"No choice."

Monica halted halfway through the door.

"Mom, why didn't you send updated pictures? He's a hunk! No wonder Michelle's moving to New Mexico."

Michelle blushed while Monica approached a smiling Randy.

"That's not why I'm going."

"The heck it isn't. He's rich and cute. I'd go too."

"Hey!" Pete said.

Randy leaped from the railing, fists clenched.

"Pete!" Everyone shouted.

He covered his mouth, while Michelle soothed Randy. After surveying the people he knew, he returned to his perch. Monica kissed her husband's bald head.

"Having a rough day, hon?"

"I liked it better here before he came. Can't be myself and you're even flirting with him."

"Aw-w. Poor Pete. If you'd been through what he has, you'd get special treatment too. Quit feeling sorry for yourself."

"I s'pose."

Monica returned her attention to Randy.

"Mom said he does whatever you tell him to."

"Not exactly," Michelle said. "He doesn't understand most of what I say. If someone can show him how to do something two or three times, he'll do it. That's how we taught him to play soft-ball."

"Good thing you found him. If someone immoral had found him, they could be teaching him all kinds of illegal things."

"Maybe. Although, I don't think we teach him as much as remind him. Everything we've ..." She used her fingers to make quotation marks in the air. "... taught him, he's done before. He knew how to use silverware, play softball, and brush his teeth. He just needed to have someone jog his memory."

"So you don't think he would have learned to steal or kill."

"Well, I wouldn't go that far. I think he would have beaten Wright to death if Chris hadn't pulled him off. It would prob-ably be easy to teach him to kill in defense of someone he cares about."

"Wow. You have a pretty awesome responsibility."

"I know."

"When are you leaving?"

Michelle sighed.

"Three weeks. His parents are flying up a couple days before."

"They have their own plane?"

"Yeah. Kendall's a pilot, but they actually have a guy who flies it for them."

"Just how rich are they?"

"I figure that's none of my business."

"What's your point?"

"They got a bunch of money," Les said. "But they don't flaunt it. Good people. They got a big ranch. Been in the family for generations. And Kendall owns three weekly and one daily newspaper. Used to have about twice that many, but decided he wanted to spend more time on the ranch."

"So they have old money."

"Yeah. Kendall didn't have to work. Neither did Randy. Got to admire men who work when they don't have to."

* * *

Michelle thought about the family gathering as she floated on her back, sunlight filtering through the trees. Randy had relaxed within an hour, even eventually roughhousing with Pete. When Randy hit several home runs during the softball game, Pete shook his fist and Randy only laughed.

She felt the water move beneath her before he gently broke the surface, lifting her with him. She wrapped her arm around his shoulders.

"You're so sensitive. You've been so careful not to scare me again."

He smiled and carried her to the blanket, where she rolled on her belly to enjoy his back rub. She tensed when he untied the strap behind her neck. *He's never done that before.* He stoked her back and neck as usual. *It's just in his way.* He only stopped after a nice, long time. Michelle sat up facing him and the straps fell, while the suit stayed in place.

She saw his curiosity before he reached for the front of her suit. *If I put it back, he'll forget it.* She did nothing. She trembled while he hesitated, then gasped when he touched her just below the collar bone. When he waited for some sign of displeasure, she tried to remain neutral with her heart pounding. He pulled the suit off her breasts.

He withdrew his hands, not risking another slap, just gazing. Michelle watched his pants. After some time, Randy lay back and closed his eyes. She let her breath out and began shaking violently. When a sob escaped, he jerked to a sitting position and held her while she exhausted herself crying. Finally, she squeezed him.

"You're a good sport. You must be so confused. I guess God sent you to me because I needed you as much as you needed me. I couldn't take these steps with anyone else. I barely trust you. I hope you still need me when you're yourself again. I love you, Randy." She pulled her suit up and he helped her retie it. "Let's snuggle for a while."

XIII.

Michelle did not recognize the car that stopped near her parents' house, but Randy knew the driver. He rushed the vehicle as the two occupants emerged. The man scrambled inside, while the woman fled. Randy ignored her, pounding on the roof above the driver's head, leaving dents. Michelle, running to catch him, finally recognized Brady.

"Randy!" She rubbed his back, but he tried the door, which Brady had locked. "Randy. Come on. He can't hurt us." He ignored her. "Brady, you'll have to leave. Go down to the highway. Someone will bring her when she's done."

Brady and the woman both scowled. Michelle reassured her.

"He hates Brady. He won't bother you."

Les and her brothers had arrived at a run. Les echoed her sentiment.

"He shouldn't of come back here. We didn't like it when he threatened Michelle. Randy just has less self-control than the rest of us. Brady, you get out of here so she can accomplish something."

The woman nodded. Brady put the car in gear and Randy walked alongside until it pointed out the driveway. He stared after it until the car could no longer be heard, then turned his glare on the woman. She stepped back. Michelle rubbed his arm.

"She won't hurt you."

His expression softened and his shoulders dropped. She patted his arm while Les welcomed their visitor.

"Sorry bout that, ma'am. Bet Brady didn't tell you how Randy reacted to him last time."

"No, sir. If I'd known that, I'd have found my own way here." She pulled out her badge. "Agent Lyons, FBI. We've taken over Captain Mc Kay's case. Detective Brady will no longer be involved."

"Good. Why didn't the FBI have it before?"

"It was treated as a murder inside Arizona. It turned into a kidnaping crossing state lines. Protocol dictates that Detective Brady should have notified the Bureau immediately."

"But he rushed up here hoping to solve the case before you got it."

"Draw your own conclusions. Is Captain Mc Kay still nonverbal?"

"Yeah. He's relaxed pretty good. We'll get back to work and let you talk to Michelle."

Michelle again reassured her.

"Come closer. Women don't bother him. You only earned his suspicion because you came with Brady. I can't believe that man was stupid enough to come back."

"This isn't typical behavior from Captain Mc Kay?"

"No. He only reacts like this if he thinks I'm threatened. Most people are considerate. It takes time to gain his trust. Not surprising considering what those animals did to him."

"Agreed. I'll get to the purpose of this trip. Two bodies were found in a remote cabin just across the Utah border. They'd been dead for some time. A single gunshot wound to the chest. They were killed with Captain Mc Kay's gun."

Michelle gasped.

"You think Randy killed them?"

"He may have. His prints were on the gun, among others. He may have gotten loose and killed them before he left the cabin."

"If he did, they deserved it. Did you find evidence that he was tortured?"

"Yes. The chair he was tied to. A strap covered in his blood. A battery and jumper cables."

"The burns on his neck?"

"Yes. They stayed in the cabin, torturing Captain Mc Kay for weeks. The last receipt recovered was dated ten days before you found him here."

"You said he *may* have killed them. Do you think there was another accomplice?"

"It's possible. I want your input. When you found Captain Mc Kay, could he have overpowered and shot two robust men in their thirties?"

"No. Even if his condition was better ten days before, the answer's the same. He couldn't hold his arms up long enough to wash his hair. Not if there was a struggle. Maybe if he just grabbed the gun and shot them."

"There was definitely a struggle."

"How were these guys connected to Randy?"

"No known connection."

"They were hired muscle?"

"Apparently."

"The person who hired them, killed them. And he's still out there."

"Possibly."

"Can he find Randy here?"

"No. The press release reported that Captain Mc Kay was found, is hospitalized and unable to relate anything about his captivity."

"We're going to his parents' ranch in a couple weeks. Will he be in danger there?"

"I hadn't been informed of that. His parents have vast resources. They will insure his safety."

"I feel safer here, but they want him home."

"Naturally, they would. I have pictures of the kidnappers. I'd like to show them to Captain Mc Kay and film his reaction."

Michelle frowned.

"Do you have to? He's been through so much."

"I understand. But until he can speak, his reaction is the only testimony we can get."

"Okay."

Agent Lyons handed Michelle two mug shots, then removed a digital camera from her pocket and aimed it at Randy.

"Anytime you're ready."

When Michelle showed him the pictures, he studied them a moment. He leaped up and backed off the porch, nearly falling. His eyes darted around and his breath came in gasps. Michelle dropped the pictures and followed him, but he backed away. His expression accused her of betrayal.

"I'm sorry, Randy. It was a bad idea. I'm sorry I hurt you."

She edged closer. But when she touched him he jerked away. She cried and he relented, letting her hug him.

"I'm so sorry."

Agent Lyons waited until Michelle returned to her chair. "You were right. But his reaction told us something very important. He doesn't have amnesia. When he recovers his ability to speak, he'll be able to tell us what happened."

"And he'll be himself again. His parents will be happy to hear that news."

XIV.

The Mc Kays arrived Wednesday, with plans to leave with Randy on Friday. They wanted to spend a day with their new friends, who they would not see for some time. Randy again hugged his parents. To Michelle's surprise, they both had a hug for her too.

Weather dictated a change of plans when clouds and rain blanketed the mountains Friday morning. Not a good day to ride to town in the back of a pickup. Saturday's forecast sounded more promising.

Kendall and Les loaded Michelle's belongings in the rented SUV as the sun broke over the mountains the next morning. Randy, obviously puzzled, helped carry boxes from her house.

"He's been wondering why I've been packing," she said. "I've told him where we're going, but he doesn't understand."

"He may be disoriented for a little while, but he'll know he's home," Kendall said. "Les, the horse haulers will come Monday for Goldie."

"No problem. I'm sure he'll miss Randy."

"Is that everything? Let's go, then. Michelle, we'll see you at the airport."

Kendall and Les left in the SUV. Bev and Liz gave them an hour so Michelle's possessions would be on the plane before Randy arrived at the airport. She and Randy snuggled in the back of the pickup, using a blanket on this cool morning.

"I'm looking forward to a milder winter. It may be tough to come back home."

Bev stopped beside the Mc Kay's twin-engine plane, raising Randy's curiosity. He drank the bottle of juice Michelle handed him. They waited on the pickup's tailgate. By the time the car dealership came for the rented SUV, his head nodded. Kendall studied him.

"You think he's ready?"

"He's pretty relaxed," Michelle said. "Let's get him up while he can still walk."

Kendall and Les put Randy between them.

"I've seen more stable drunks. Michelle, get in the plane so he can see you. Even in this condition, he might balk about going in."

The three nearly dragged Randy inside, not because he balked, but because he was dead weight. They lay him on a couch along one side of the plane. The pilot appeared from his hiding place and began his pre-flight check while Michelle said her good byes.

"Liz will give me a cell phone so I can call anytime."

"I'm counting on that," Bev said. "Enjoy the winter and re-member to take care of yourself while you're taking care of Randy. Now, go before I cry."

Michelle hugged her parents and climbed aboard, taking a seat across the narrow aisle from Randy. Kendall closed the door, then took his place as co-pilot. Liz turned in her seat.

"Ever been in a plane this small?"

"Never been in a plane."

"Oh, my. Kendall and Jerry are both good pilots, with lots of hours in this plane."

"Is Randy a pilot too?"

"No. He's not fond of flying. I don't know how he got the nerve to take sky diving lessons."

"Does he still do that?"

"No. I don't think he did it again after he finished the lessons. He wanted to be qualified as a smoke jumper. But he got the job in Arizona instead. Thank God."

"Amen to that."

Liz faced forward to hide her smile when the plane began moving.

Michelle gripped the arms of her seat during takeoff, then tried to relax as the plane headed east out of the mountains before turning south for the three-hour flight. Randy barely moved.

Finally, Liz pointed out a right side window.

"There's Wheeler Peak. It's just north of Taos. Full of ski areas. We're getting close." A few minutes later, she indicated another mountain. "Middle Truchas Peak. Straight west of the ranch."

On the plane's descent, Michelle noticed the valleys covered with fields and the forested higher elevations. The pilot buzzed the sprawling ranch yard carved out of the forest before making his approach to the landing strip in the valley below. When the plane touched down, the wheels kicked up dust on the paved runway. The pilot stopped in front of a hanger containing a smaller plane and an old jeep. Evergreen-covered hills rose behind the building.

An extended cab pickup arrived before the pilot cut the engines. When Kendall opened the door, Randy rolled over, but slept on. He opened his eyes several times while they unloaded baggage. Kendall and Jerry heaved him out of the plane, and the ranch foreman, Sam, helped get him to the bed of the pickup.

Michelle sat with Randy as the pickup climbed the gently sloping, mile long, dusty road to the ranch yard. They rounded a bend and the buildings spread out before them. She whistled.

"Nice place."

A huge house surrounded by an expanse of green lawn looked down on barns, stables, machine shops, and numerous other buildings. White pipe fences surrounded the lawn and formed several corrals.

Sam drove around the house to the guesthouse beside the swimming pool. He and Kendall helped a rubbery-legged Randy to a cot on the porch. Michelle carried in her possessions until he sat up, groggy and confused. She joined him, rubbing his back.

"You're home, Randy."

He blinked and yawned. Liz hovered just off the porch.

"I'll have Elena bring us some lemonade."

She departed. Randy yawned again, but sat up straighter when Sam walked to the pickup for another box. He watched him return, tensing as he passed. When Sam came from the house again, Michelle stopped him.

"Thanks, Sam. That'll have to be your last trip. He's getting his defenses up."

Sam nodded and let Kendal finish before driving away. Liz returned and placed the tray of lemonade on a patio table. When Michelle handed Randy a glass, he gulped it.

"He's dehydrated from the flight," Kendal said. "He looks confused, but some of that's the drug hangover. This should start looking familiar. If he doesn't settle down before, he will when Goldie gets here."

"I'll stay with him as much as I can."

"I think we should leave you to settle in. We'll be able to see Randy every day now, but it'll be best if we let you develop your routine. Elena will bring dinner at seven. There are snack foods and beverages in the kitchen. You can discuss meal schedules with her." He stood, but Liz hesitated. "Come on, Liz. He isn't going anywhere."

Randy watched them go, then leaned against the wall, looking around. Michelle sat with him until she absolutely had to go inside. He followed without hesitation. When she closed the bathroom door between them, he leaned against it and slid to the floor. He sat there with tear-stained cheeks until she came out.

She led him to the sofa and he lay with his head on her thigh while she stoked his hair.

"You've had a rough day. But this is nothing compared to some of the things you've been through. I'll be here for you."

* * *

During the day, Michelle familiarized herself with the spacious guest house and walked around the ranch yard, always with Randy glued to her. She avoided several workers, seeking the company of horses instead. These responded to him much as Goldie had. His body relaxed.

They snacked on cheese, crackers, and fresh vegetables to tide them over until supper, what they called dinner here.

"We'll have to ask Elena if she can feed us earlier. We only ate that late when we were busy in the hay field." As if on cue, someone knocked on the door, unnerving Randy. "It's okay. At least she knocked."

She opened the door for the Hispanic woman about her age, holding a tray. The dishes rattled.

"Dinner for you and Mr. Randall, ma'am."

Michelle took the tray, concerned that Elena would drop it. "Call me Michelle. We'll fend for ourselves for breakfast."

"Yes, ma'am."

"Have you always been afraid of Randy?"

Elena's eyes widened.

"Oh, no, ma'am. He was a very nice man. I've just heard Mrs. Liz and Mr. Kendall talking about what he's like now."

"He's still a nice man. Men make him nervous, but he gets along great with women. If you let him know you're coming, there's no reason to be afraid."

"Thank you, ma'am. Excuse me."

Michelle set the tray on the table and raised the covers. "Not my usual grub. Looks pretty southwestern. And it smells delicious."

Salad, quesadillas, some kind of enchilada, fruit, and salsa. Randy ate with his usual enthusiasm.

"Do you put salsa on everything?" He only spared the fruit.

He polished off his food before she half-finished, then eyed hers. "Don't even think about it. Elena's a great cook. I want these enchiladas for myself. I'll tell her to bring you twice as much next time."

When his eyes nearly begged, she retrieved a pint of ice cream from the freezer to keep him busy until she finished.

While loading the dishwasher, she wondered what Randy would do at bedtime. He had finally relaxed enough to allow up to ten feet between them, only becoming distressed when she shut the bathroom door in his face.

"No time like the present. I'm tired from that trip. I'm going to bed early." He followed her into the bedroom. "At least you've already seen most of me."

He watched her remove her blouse and bra, then pull on the long T-shirt she wore to bed. She unzipped her jeans and slid them off, before crossing the hall to the bathroom. She handed him his toothbrush and they both brushed their teeth. When she shut him out, he stayed on his feet and tear-free.

He waited until she returned to the bedroom, then used the bathroom without closing the door.

"Typical man." She climbed into the king-size bed. After removing his shirt and jeans, he crawled under the covers and wrapped his arms around her waist. "Um-m. I could get used to this."

XV.

Michelle slept the next morning until Randy stirred. She dressed, not knowing when to expect visitors. But no one knocked on her door. She took her third cup of coffee to the porch. Liz appeared from the big house, strolling around the pool with her travel mug.

"Good morning. How'd you sleep?"

"Like a log. Very comfortable bed."

"Where did Randy sleep?"

"With me. He won't leave my side."

"That doesn't bother you?"

"No. I had to snuggle up to him when it stormed. He's a good snuggler."

"Where did you undress?"

Michelle blushed.

"I've had to get over being shy. He doesn't give me much privacy."

"Have you been away from him since he came to your ranch?"

"No. I guess I haven't. No farther than inside my house, anyhow."

"Hopefully, he can get comfortable enough here to let you have some space. You need time to yourself."

"I don't mind, really. I enjoy being with Randy."

"I see that. But you'll like it even more with a little breathing room." Liz sipped coffee. "Seeing you undress doesn't excite him at all?"

"If it did, I wouldn't do it in front of him."

Liz gazed at her son and sighed.

"Oh, Randy. Will you ever be yourself again?"

"He will, Liz. I know it."

"Thanks for being so positive. I wish I could be. It's just that ... we've waited so long for that heir to carry on the Mc Kay name. Every time we started to hope that he'd finally found a wife, he'd break up with her. We love all our grandchildren, but we need that heir."

"I think I understand."

"You must love kids, given your profession."

"Good thing I do. There aren't many careers that would have let me live on the ranch."

"But you don't get many chances to meet a husband."

"That used to be fine with me. I wasn't interested in marriage."

"What changed your mind?"

"Randy. He's gotten me over my fear of men."

"Your mom told me you were sexually assaulted. I'm amazed that you've been able to handle Randy's attention."

"It helped that he was so timid at first. There have been bumps. He'd make a sudden move and I'd start shaking. But he hates to upset me. Once he figures out what bothers me, he avoids it."

"Perhaps you've both come a long way."

"Yes. I suppose so."

"Hopefully, he can continue to help you."

Michelle wondered about that comment, but changed the subject. "You know, this is a pretty easy job. I don't have to set an alarm. I can keep my summer schedule year round."

Liz laughed.

"That's fine. You earn your pay just being with Randy. We've spoken to a psychologist friend about continuing Randy's treatment. She plans to give him a couple weeks to settle in, then spend an entire day with you to decide her course of action. And don't worry, she sees you as a friend, not a foe."

"Good. Will she tell me when she's coming?"

"Absolutely."

* * *

"Come on, Randy, you need a bath." She turned off the water in the massive tub. "There isn't enough privacy here to take one outside. Besides, before long, it'll be too cold. You need to get used to taking one in here."

She started unbuttoning his shirt. Understanding, he finished undressing. She nudged him toward the tub, but he balked. Several tries produced the same results. She studied him with her hands on her hips.

"I don't get it. You're not afraid. You must understand what I have in mind. Unless. Has the concept of taking a bath inside become completely foreign to you?" She nodded. "I'll bet that's it. You don't remember that people take bathes inside. I have to remind you." She bit her lip. "Well, here goes."

He watched her remove her blouse and bra. With trembling hands, she pushed her jeans off. And, finally, her underwear. She looked up at Randy, staring wide-eyed at her anatomy.

"Surprise. There's something else different."

After a moment, he dropped to his knees for a closer look. She jumped back, then tried to relax. She took a step toward him and patted his shoulder.

"I hope you're just curious. Please, don't get turned on."

She gasped when he placed his hands on her waist. He slid them over her hips, then to her thighs. Michelle felt a rush of warmth through her body. She still trembled, but not from fear.

"Forget what I said about not getting turned on."

His hands returned to her waist, producing a shudder. When

he looked up to see if that was good or bad, she smiled. He stood, his curiosity satisfied. She sighed.

"Oh, well. It was just a thought. This is better for my conscience anyway."

She climbed into the tub and gestured for him to follow. No hesitation this time. Though they both fit, she had not planned for the volume of water two bodies would displace. She drained a little to prevent a flood.

"There. Now you get a chance to wash my back like I wash yours. This might actually be fun."

* * *

After two uneventful days on the ranch, Michelle and Randy relaxed on the porch in the afternoon. She sighed, gazing at the beautiful, clear blue sky. She had yet to see a cloud in New Mexico.

Someone appeared beside the porch, startling her.

Randy bolted from his chair, vaulted the railing, and pursued the person around the house. Michelle used the stairs and rounded the porch in time to see Sergio, the gardener, back himself into a corner. With no place to go, Sergio could not leave Randy's space. The man looked as frightened as Michelle felt.

She tugged on Randy's arm.

"Randy, no!"

He shrugged her off. She heard Elena shriek by the kitchen door.

"Mrs. Liz! Mr. Randall's attacking Sergio!"

Michelle put herself between Randy and Sergio, a space that had shrunk to six feet. Randy pushed her behind him. She fell with a little yelp. He whirled and crouched beside her. With his attention diverted, Sergio ran.

Randy stroked her hair, then wrapped his arms around her, pressing his cheek against hers. When he scooped her up, she saw Liz running from the house.

"Michelle! What happened? Are you hurt?"

"I'm fine. He had Sergio cornered. Nothing else worked, so I fell down to distract him. But he thinks he hurt me. He feels terrible."

Randy nuzzled her, breathing on her neck.

"He loves you."

"I think he's adopted me."

"What brought this on?"

"Sergio just appeared beside the porch. I didn't hear him. He surprised me. Randy reacted like you'd expect him to."

"We warned the entire staff about surprising him. This *won't* happen again. I'll let Kendall deal with Sergio when he gets home. Randy, you can put her down."

He showed no inclination to release Michelle, who wiggled to encourage him. He took a more secure hold.

"He's strong." She pointed at the porch and he carried her there, sitting with her on his lap. He pressed his face into her hair. "I wonder how long this will last. Guess I'll only fall down in an emergency."

"It would have served Sergio right to get a good thrashing, but we know how far Randy can go. You did the right thing."

Michelle persisted in trying to rise, and he finally let her. He looked her up and down, then hid his face between her breasts. Her heart raced, but she comforted him.

"It's okay. You didn't hurt me."

"He's taking this very hard. But that's okay. Don't let it bother you."

"I'll try not to. It just breaks my heart when his feelings are hurt."

XVI.

Blonde, bronzed, and beautiful, she hesitated beside the blue sports car. Then, to Michelle's horror, she ran toward Randy. Michelle watched, speechless, as the woman threw her arms around his neck. He stepped back, but she clung to him. Forcibly, but gently, he pried himself loose. The life-sized Barbie doll began crying.

"Randy, honey. It's me, Robin. I love you, Randy."

Michelle stiffened, but tried not to let her voice reflect it.

"He didn't even know his parents when he first saw them."

"Oh. Well, that doesn't matter. I'll be here for him. I'll quit my job if I have to. When you love someone, you make sacrifices."

"You'll have to talk to his parents about that. Here comes Liz now."

"Robin," Liz said. "I told you he's not ready."

"I couldn't stay away, Liz. I just had to see him. I love him so much."

Liz sighed.

"Give him space. He's doing better with you than he did with us."

"Maybe he remembers me. Do you, Randy?" He stepped behind Michelle and wrapped an arm around her shoulders. Robin's lip quivered. "Maybe you were right, Liz. This is tough to see. But if I stay away, how will he remember me?"

"I understand. I'll have Elena bring refreshments to the pool. We'll let him get reacquainted with you."

Michelle led Randy to a love seat pool-side. He surprised her by snuggling. Robin glared until Liz returned. She stared at her son.

"Is that his idea?"

"Absolutely. Maybe Robin scared him."

"How could I scare him?"

"By running at him. He can't handle pushy people."

"I wasn't pushy. I was just so happy to see him. You *could* discourage him from hanging on you like that."

"My job is to encourage him."

"I'll bet you do it well."

Liz cleared her throat.

"Without Michelle, Randy would have been institutionalized. What she's doing works."

"I can see that. If she could teach me what she does, I could take care of him. He should be in the care of people who love him."

"We'll talk about it. But we won't rush into anything."

✳ ✳ ✳

Michelle wanted to hit her. Unless Robin had a black belt, she thought she could take her. Michelle had been led to this desperate state by her inability to talk to Liz without Robin present. Robin stuck to Randy and Randy stuck to Michelle.

She set her alarm the next morning, hoping that Robin slept in. Randy seemed puzzled when she dressed before her first cup of coffee.

"I *have* to talk to your mom. Robin's trying to pull a fast one. I have to tell Liz what your friend, Carlos, said about her. Before she can get her hooks in you. She thinks no one knows that you broke up with her, including you. I'll bet she'd have no qualms about seducing you."

She filled their travel mugs and walked around the pool to the main house. When she knocked on the kitchen door, Elena waved her in.

"Good morning, Michelle. He's following you in real good now."

"He learns fast with the right motivation. Is Liz around yet?"

"I haven't seen her, but she's up. Mr. Kendall left early."

"How about *Robin*?"

Elena smirked.

"Don't know. I see you like her as much as I do."

"Less. She's another gold digger. I need to find a way to talk to Liz without Robin around. That's why I'm here so early. Hope she sleeps in."

But before long, they heard voices. When Robin saw Randy sitting on the kitchen stool, she wrapped her tentacles around him. He squirmed, then submitted. While Liz retrieved coffee, Robin slid her hand between Randy's legs. He giggled and Michelle fumed.

When her eyes met Elena's, the latter acted.

"Mr. Randall, I'll bet you'd like a nice big breakfast of pancakes and juevos rancheros, wouldn't you."

Randy lost interest in Robin. He liked pancakes more than ice cream and recognized the word. He watched Elena take the griddle down from the rack above the kitchen island, and grinned when she brought the batter from the refrigerator.

Michelle poured him more coffee and stood at his elbow, cramping Robin's technique, until Elena set a plate in front of him. He would not notice Robin's seduction with food to consume. Michelle signaled Liz to join her in another room. Liz complied.

"I'm sorry, Michelle. I know you don't like Robin much, and she is a bit pushy. But it wouldn't be fair to Randy to keep her away. She obviously loves him."

"Or his money."

"He wouldn't have asked her to move in with him if she was after his money."

"Did he?"

"What?"

"Did he tell you that, before he was kidnapped?"

"No. Robin told us."

"Do you know his friend Carlos?"

"Of course. Carlos came home with Randy several times."

"Ask him about Robin."

"Why? What did he tell you?"

"I may be confused. Let him tell you. In the meantime, I'll try to keep Robin out of Randy's pants."

"Yes. Do that. We don't need her getting pregnant if she's a gold digger. A baby would give her access to the family fortune. Interfere as much as necessary."

Michelle hurried back to the kitchen and found Randy devouring pancakes and eggs while Robin kept her hand busy under the kitchen counter. Michelle could see her frustration as he cast her no more than an occasional glance.

"Robin, how'd you sleep last night?"

"Not well at all. I couldn't stop thinking about Randy. We have a long road ahead of us. But he's worth it."

"Yeah, he's worth a lot. Keep your hands to yourself."

"I beg your pardon."

"Quit teasing him."

"Mind your own business. Randy's a big boy. We've done this before."

"Then he had a choice. You can come on to him again when he tells me it's okay."

"You won't be around that long."

"One of us won't. Keep your hand to yourself or I'll break it."

Robin withdrew her hand.

"Don't think I won't tell Liz about this when she gets back."

"Good luck with that."

Michelle drank coffee and Elena busied herself at the griddle, trying to hide a smile. Randy kept eating, oblivious to the tense silence. Twenty minutes passed before Liz returned, her scowl reflecting what she had just heard.

"Liz, you won't believe ..."

"Shut up, Robin! You have some nerve. How dare you try to endear yourself to us when we were vulnerable! You used Randy's kidnaping to try and get your hands on his money. How dare you!"

"Liz, what are you talking about? I love Randy."

"You love his money. Randy broke up with you just before he disappeared."

"That's a lie. Who told you that?"

"Carlos."

Robin hesitated. Her scam had been discovered, but she did not give up.

"We were going through a rough time. But we would have worked it out."

"Get out! You have five minutes to pack your things and get out, or I'll have you forcibly removed. If you ever come back, I'll have you arrested."

Robin surrendered. Liz followed her and Michelle let her breath out. Randy resumed eating. Elena smiled.

"That even got Mr. Randall's attention."

Michelle stroked his hair and kissed his cheek.

"You're safe. We won't let any gold diggers get you."

Liz returned after closing the door behind Robin.

"Thank, God. I never really liked that woman. Thanks for exposing her."

"Thank Carlos. I would've been in the dark if he hadn't said something."

"But you had the courage to speak up. I told Carlos I'd call back to thank him properly. Elena, did Randy eat all the pancakes? I've worked up an appetite."

XVII

Liz introduced Dr. Lopez to Michelle and Randy, then left them by the pool. Dr. Lopez first insisted that Michelle call her "Carla," then told her to go about her routine. Michelle did her best, even finding a chair for her while they rode. Randy seemed puzzled that they stayed near the buildings rather than riding into the mountains.

After lunch, Carla had a request.

"He recognizes quite a few words. Would you do me a favor and teach him a new one?"

"Oh. That means I have to think of something he'll want. He won't pay attention if he's not motivated. 'Eat' and 'drink' were easy. So were 'bath, swim, and ride.' What would he want now?"

"Good point. He just ate, or I'd ask you to work on a specific food."

Michelle grinned and walked to the freezer.

"Randy's never full. Randy, want some ice cream?" His name caught his attention. She pulled a carton from the freezer and he smiled. "Ice cream?" He smiled and she retrieved a spoon. "Ice cream?" She handed him the spoon, but withheld the treat. He scowled. "Ice cream?"

He reached for it and she let him take a spoonful, then withdrew. He glared at her.

"Ice cream?" He reached for it again and she let him eat more before backing away. "Ice cream?" He smiled and reached for it and she handed him the carton. "There. When he smiles, he gets it. Most things, he figures out in two or three tries."

"The trauma obviously hasn't affected his intelligence. I can't explain why he doesn't automatically pick up everything you say. For some reason there's a short circuit in his ability to learn."

"I don't even feel like I'm teaching him, just reminding him. When he smiles, it's like the light bulb going on. Like, 'Oh, yeah. I remember.' I don't know how to teach him to talk."

"Don't worry about that. But start teaching him as many words as you can. He's capable."

"I should have thought of that sooner. I'll make up lesson plans like I did for my students."

"Excellent. Your background makes you an ideal teacher for him. Now I'll broach a more delicate matter. Has Liz expressed her concern about his inactive libido?"

"Several times."

"How do you feel about that?"

"Relieved. I couldn't help him if I had to fight him off. He would have ended up in an institution."

"I'll remind Liz of that. I'm sympathetic. She nearly lost her son with no grandson to carry on the family name. So her concern is understandable. Tell me about his lack of libido. What doesn't he react to that you would expect? Give me some examples of stimuli which don't cause a reaction.

"Well." Michelle stroked his hair while he devoured the ice cream. "I hope I don't shock you. Since we moved here, he's been sleeping with me."

"I see. Go on."

"He really doesn't give me much privacy. I change clothes in front of him." Carla's eyes widened. "And I couldn't get him in the bathtub here until I was taking a bath."

"Oh, my. Does Liz know all this?"

"Most of it."

"No wonder she's concerned. All I can tell her is to be patient. I believe it will come. But do you realize that when it does, you will probably be the object of his affection?"

"It's occurred to me. I'm not concerned. I'm not a psychologist, but I have a theory."

"You know him best. I'd like to hear it."

"Even the most basic things like eating with silverware and brushing his teeth, I've had to show him two or three times." She blushed. "I think sex would be the same. Unfortunately, there's only one way to prove that theory."

"Seduce him. Not a wise course of action. But your theory has merit. I'll tell Liz about that too. Based on his improvement since Dr. Fontaine's early observations, I have every reason to feel optimistic that he will recover fully."

"That's how I feel."

"Even better. Since you're with him daily, progress would be harder to see. I'll give Liz an update now and come back in a month. I'll only need a couple hours with him next time. Keep up the good work."

* * *

Randy learned fast if Michelle could motivate him. In no time, he recognized the names of foods and beverages, items related to horses and nature. But his mind wandered when she tried to interest him in articles of clothing, colors, or nearly anything else.

"Almost every teacher has this problem. At least I only have one student to motivate. Let's make this a game."

She led him to the bathroom.

"Take your shirt off." She tugged at it. "Shirt. Take your shirt off." He removed it. "Now take my shirt off. Shirt." She patted it and raised her arms. He smiled and pulled her T-shirt off. She hugged him. "Good."

She sat and began unlacing her boots.

"Now your boots. Take your boots off." He imitated her, still smiling. "I think games will work with you. "Take your jeans off." She slapped his hip and he complied. "Now my jeans."

She gasped and gripped his biceps when he did her bidding. He worked his fingers under the sides of her sports bra, but she clamped her arms on his hands.

"No. Not until I tell you to. Okay. Now the bra."

She raised her arms. He moved with care, not wanting his fingers slapped again.

"Now the underwear." He finished undressing without a signal from her, then removed hers. Michelle studied him. "Did you understand that, or have you just figured out the game?"

After starting the shower, she stepped in and he joined her.

"Good thing this isn't one of those tiny stalls. Get the soap." He already knew that word. She held out her hand. "Give me the soap." He complied. "Let's wash your back." She nudged him to turn around and repeated the phrase while she worked. "There. Now wash my back."

She handed him the soap and turned. He began, drawing a gasp from her. She pressed her hands against the wall as he progressed. When he reached the small of her back, her groan made him pause. Then he chuckled and continued much longer than needed.

"Oh, I *like* this game." She faced him. "That wasn't my intention. I really thought you'd learn better. And I was right. So if you learn and I enjoy myself, it's okay. Right?"

Randy smiled as if he understood. She continued teaching him body parts, hands, arms, and shoulders, as they washed each other. Moving with great care, she said the next word.

"Chest."

She slid her hand from his shoulder to his chest. His muscles tightened and he frowned.

"Chest. I know. You think I'm not supposed to touch your chest. You haven't forgotten that hand slap. But I'm teaching now. Chest."

He relaxed.

"Good. Now, do I have the nerve to ask you to do the same? Chest."

She guided his hand, but he pulled away. After three more failed attempts, she accepted his decision.

"Okay. You really don't want to take any chances. Stomach."

His smile returned while each washed the other's belly. When she hesitated, he moved her soapy hand across his hip.

"You want to learn more. Hip." She repeated it as she washed the other hip. "Leg." She kneeled and washed his legs, using care not to go too far, watching for a reaction. "Even that doesn't turn you on. We won't tell your mom about this. She doesn't need another reason to worry."

When she rose, he took the soap from her and waited for instructions.

"Oh, my. Hip." He washed while she directed him. She caught her breath when he dropped to his knees. He chuckled and exercised far less care while washing her legs. She dug her fingers into his shoulders. He again took his time. When he stood, she leaned against him. "You could have your way with me. I've never wanted anyone like this."

XVIII.

"Randy," his sister, Rachel, said edging toward him. She fought back tears. "Do you remember me?"

He accepted her hug and she stopped fighting. She sobbed while her husband and four children waited. When she finally turned him loose, the children mobbed Randy, to his delight.

"He loves kids, doesn't he," Michelle said.

"He's always been great with them. Thanks for rescuing my baby brother."

"I don't think I rescued him."

"Don't belittle your accomplishment. You saved his life. And Mom says he's come a long way with your care. We're all grateful."

"It's the easiest job I've ever had. I enjoy his company. He's a good listener."

Rachel laughed.

"Randy's never had much to say. But it wouldn't surprise me if we won't be able to shut him up once he starts talking."

"We're looking forward to that," Liz said.

They visited by the pool while Randy wrestled with the two younger kids. The older ones excused themselves to ride horses. Michelle sensed that Rachel held back until her mother left to check on dinner.

"Mom says that Randy sleeps with you."

"Yes."

"And there's nothing?"

"That's a pretty vague question, but no."

Rachel sighed.

"I guess that's good for your sake. But it's sad. It's not like Randy. My parents had to deal with two paternity suits when he was in high school. The girls were just looking for a rich father for their babies, but Randy never denied that he could have done the deed."

"He was like *that?*"

Rachel chuckled.

"He changed after that first summer fighting fires. He learned to give instead of take. Kids, you're wearing out Uncle Randy. Why don't you get your suits and go for a swim." They ran to change while Randy grabbed a glass of lemonade and sat beside Michelle. Rachel sipped her drink. "When Randy's ready to travel, bring him up to see us. He should feel safe there."

"I haven't even tried getting him inside a vehicle."

"There are plenty here. No reason you can't use one. Right, Mom?"

Liz returned to her seat.

"Vehicles? Yes. I'm sorry, Michelle. I should have thought of that. You must feel like a prisoner here."

"No. I feel less isolated than I did at home."

"Still, you need to be able to leave if you want to. The blue Explorer is yours to use. You know where the gas pump is. Fill it there and go where you please."

"If I can get Randy inside."

"He wants to be with you," Rachel said. "Get in and drive away. He'll come."

"That almost sounds cruel."

"He's smart. He'll get the message."

The kids ran out and jumped in the pool. Randy pointed, but Michelle just smiled.

"You can go swimming without me. Go change." She waved him toward the guest house. "Go for a swim." He stood and took a step, then looked back. She waved again. "Go on."

He drifted toward the house, looking over his shoulder, and hesitated at the door before entering. Liz clapped her hands.

"Oh, that's such a big step."

Michelle wiped a tear away.

"Amazing. He's acting like an adult."

* * *

Susan blew in the next afternoon, followed dutifully by her husband and 18-year-old son. Cigarette in hand, she marched toward Randy. He stepped back as she advanced. She kept coming and he took another step back. Michelle intervened.

"When he runs out of space, he'll defend himself."

"You must be the nursemaid." Susan blew smoke without bothering to look at Michelle. "Is that right? Are you dangerous, little brother? Do you need to be locked up where you can't hurt anybody?"

"Susan." Kendall said. "That will do. It was bad enough that you goaded him when he could defend himself. Have a little compassion for what your brother's been through."

She snorted.

"The rest of you have more than enough compassion. You've always made allowances for him."

She pushed within a foot of Randy. His expression hardened and he quit retreating. He grabbed her cigarette and crushed it out in his hand, his eyes reflecting disdain. She poked her forefinger into his chest.

"Well, little brother, maybe you still have stones." She glanced at Michelle. "Does he, nursemaid? You getting any?"

Michelle clenched her fists and her teeth, but Kendall responded.

"Susan! Remember, this gathering is to celebrate your brother's homecoming. Try to get in the spirit of the occasion."

She pulled out another cigarette.

"Whatever. I need a drink."

She stalked into the next room, followed by her two-man parade.

"What a charming woman," Michelle said.

Rachel laughed.

"Bet you thought she couldn't be as bad as we said."

"Rachel," Kendall said. "It's not all that funny. After all Randy's been through, you'd think she could muster a little compassion."

"Maybe I'm more realistic because she's my sister, not my daughter. I didn't think she would. He doesn't like her any more than she likes him."

Michelle tried to place a positive slant on the confrontation.

"Did you see him? He didn't let her intimidate him."

"He acted like Randy," Kendall said. "Just without the words he usually flings at her. As much as I hate to see their confrontations, having him cower from Susan would've been worse."

* * *

Michelle sipped her coffee.

"By this time of year at home, it would be too cool to drink our morning coffee on the porch." Randy smiled. "I like it here. I just miss the smell of the evergreens. They were so close at home. I guess if I get really homesick, I can walk a couple hundred yards. These aren't spruce trees, but they'll do."

Susan stepped out the patio doors, saw them, and marched around the pool. Michelle groaned. Susan sneered.

"Good morning, nursemaid. How are you and the trained monkey this morning?"

"My name is Michelle Bowman."

"As if I care." She stood over Randy. "Just how far would I have to push him before he pushed back?"

"He's not the animal you think he is."

Susan stomped on Randy's foot. He leaped up, bumping her. She smirked.

"Did I make you mad, little brother?"

Michelle set her coffee aside and rose.

"He may not be quite as mad as I am. Leave! You're not welcome here."

"Ha! I'm the *Mc Kay* and you're the *employee*. You don't tell me what to do."

"Wrong. Your parents told me to treat this house like my own. Leave!"

Susan noticed that the confrontation with Michelle had further agitated Randy. She pushed, directing her venom at Michelle, but maintaining the physical confrontation with him.

"I won't be ordered around by a bumpkin who thinks she can endear herself to my parents by taking care of their mindless wonder. You just want to get your hooks in their money."

Randy clenched his fists, but Michelle moved. She seized Susan's wrist, twisted her arm behind her back, and propelled her off the porch. Before she could recover, Michelle and Randy had entered the house. Michelle locked the door and listened to Susan screaming expletives.

Randy grinned and hugged her.

"Don't encourage me. I have a temper."

XIX.

For what must have been the tenth time Michelle drove 100 feet, then stopped. Randy jogged after her and gazed in the open passenger door. She sighed.

"Okay. You asked for it."

This time she drove a hundred yards. When he reached her, she only paused briefly before advancing the same distance. This time when he caught up, he had broken a sweat. She drove on. When he caught her, she took her foot off the brake. He jumped in, leaving the door open. She smiled and crept past the landing strip.

"We'll have to clean the inside of this when we get done. We're letting in an awful lot of dust."

He finally closed the door and she accelerated. Fields flanked either side of the straight road. It curved once when the valley took a turn. The ridges on either side gave way to a larger valley. She reached the highway and a sign informing visitors that they had a five-mile drive to the M C K Ranch. She saw only fields for a mile in either direction.

"This must by Highway 518. If we turn left, Taos is 40 miles or so. But I think this is far enough for your first ride."

She made a u-turn and returned to the ranch, finding Liz waiting by the garage.

"How far before he got in?"

"Almost to the landing strip. I had to tire him out."

"Wonderful. When will you visit Rachel?"

"We'll take rides for a week before we tackle that."

"You're so patient with him. We appreciate you so much."

"Thanks. Now we need to vacuum the dust out of here."

"Someone can do that for you."

"A little work will be good for us."

"Okay. But join me for lunch when you finish."

* * *

When Elena showed them to the formal dining room, Michelle wondered if Liz considered this a celebration. She and Kendall usually ate in the dining area just off the kitchen. Liz said little and fidgeted until Elena served the fried ice cream.

"That will be all, Elena. We'll clear the table ourselves." Elena departed. "She serves Randy double of everything."

"Keeps him from eating my food."

"But he's not getting fat."

"No. He gets plenty of exercise. And he's eating less between meals."

"Good. He's never had a weight problem. I'd hate to see that happen."

"I don't think you have to worry."

"I have enough things to worry about. Like him not having children."

"That really bothers you, doesn't it?"

"He's almost thirty years old. I worried about it before those animals took him. We thought we'd lost him. He needs to father children."

"He will."

"You could help with that."

Michelle stopped with her spoon halfway to her mouth.

"Excuse me."

"You said he learns if you show him two or three times. Show him."

Michelle blushed.

"Are you asking me to seduce him?"

"No. Just remind him of what he already knows. He'll appreciate it."

"I'm sorry, Liz. No matter what kind of spin you put on it, I'd be seducing him."

"I suppose. Technically. But he'll be glad you did."

"Liz, you may be asking the impossible." She hesitated, then decided to omit nothing. "We shower together. We even wash each other sometimes. Nothing happens."

"Oh. Do you wash all of him?"

Michelle's face reddened more.

"No."

"Maybe you should." She gave her a moment. "If you have his child, you'll never have to work again. You won't need to worry about finding a job after your nieces and nephews get older."

"I'm not after his money!"

"I know. I wouldn't suggest this if you were. You love him. Do this for him."

Michelle bit her lip, then sighed.

"Let's not rush into anything. Let's think about this for a week and discuss it again."

"Of course. I wouldn't expect less from you. This isn't a decision that should be made lightly. But I won't change my mind. I've thought about this for weeks. It wasn't easy for me to get up the nerve to ask you. You're the right woman for him."

"Shouldn't he make that decision."

"I've seen the way he looks at you. I think he already has."

Michelle studied Randy, scraping the last spoonful of ice cream from his bowl. He smiled at her. *Liz sees what she wants to see.*

* * *

While Michelle continued taking Randy for drives and teaching him word associations, she could not stop thinking about Liz's proposal. *Or was it a proposition?* In the shower, her body implored her to accept the offer. She dug her fingers into his shoulders, panting. He chuckled and wrapped his arms around her.

"M-m. You like to see me enjoying myself. Do you want me to make you just as happy? Your mom thinks I should. But it's wrong. I don't know how I can get past that." He stroked the small of her back, bringing a shudder. "That could do it. How about if we dry off and I remind you how to kiss?"

She sat cross-legged on the bed and patted the area in front of her. Noticing his puzzled expression, she smiled.

"Naked kissing is more effective."

She kissed the palm of his hand, then held up hers for him to reciprocate. He smiled and licked it. She kissed his hand again, this time turning it to give him a better view. He managed an approximation of a kiss. She showed him a third time and he mastered the technique.

"Three times, just like always. Let's try some other spots."

They traded kisses. Arms, then shoulders, neck, cheeks. He enjoyed the game, though not as much as Michelle did. She kept her first kiss to his lips quick. He chuckled. The next time, she used her tongue and he jerked back.

"Was that a surprise? Give it time. You'll like it."

When she tried another kiss, he withdrew. She laughed and teased him, bobbing and weaving like a boxer. When he grinned, she tried again. This time, he allowed it to work. After a few seconds, he pulled her against him, lay back, and rolled over with her.

She tensed. *Have I found the right button to push? I wasn't planning to seduce him.* But her concern vanished when nothing else happened. *He just likes kissing.*

He stopped to catch his breath and she sighed.

"I think your mom expects the impossible. Just as well. I believe I should wait for sex until after marriage. You're not ready for wedding vows."

He kissed her again, eventually moving to her neck. Michelle shrieked.

"You figured that out on your own."

* * *

Because so many unfamiliar vehicles entered the ranch yard, Michelle and Randy had learned to ignore them. But Michelle noticed when the dark-haired man stared, then strolled in their direction. Her eyes darted to the inscription on the window of his mini-van, "United Fire Equipment." He smiled.

"Randy, how are you, buddy?"

"He won't remember you. He hasn't remembered anybody. Just keep moving slowly and don't come too close."

"I shouldn't have come. But I was traveling through, and I've been thinking a lot about him. I'm Dom Martini. Randy and I got to know each other through my job. We got to be friends because we both like horses."

He handed her a business card, which she grasped by the edges, glanced at, then held behind her back.

"His parents never mentioned you."

"I've never had the pleasure. I travel a lot. When I was in the Phoenix area, we'd go for a ride. Not something I get to do much when I'm on the road. So, how is he?"

"Physically fine. Still can't communicate or understand what we say."

"But he's tense, like he's waiting for me to make a move."

"He's always that way with new people. He takes a while to trust."

"Not surprising. You think he'll ever be the old Randy again?"

"I don't know. How do you recover from something like that?"

"Yeah. At least he's alive. I'll get out of here. I won't bother you again. If he gets better, you can tell him I was here."

"Thanks for stopping."

Michelle waited until he drove away, carried the card into the house and dropped it in a plastic bag. She punched Agent Lyons number on speed dial and reached her voice mail.

"Randy had a visitor today who claimed to be a friend. I have his fingerprints."

* * *

Agent Lyons arrived the next day to collect the business card.

"Your suspicions were justified. There is a 'United Fire Equipment,' but they have no employee named Dom Martini. I hope you have good prints."

"You should have a good thumb and index finger from his right hand. Have you found anything on Randy's ex-girlfriend?"

Agent Lyons tried to suppress a smile.

"We've found no connection to Captain Mc Kay's kidnappers. She's committed no crime. If you hadn't been here to stop her, she probably would have. But nothing more serious than fraud."

Michelle sighed.

"I really wanted it to be her. But she probably doesn't have the stomach for what they did to Randy. She would have kidnapped him for ransom. Have you made any progress?"

"I'm afraid I can't share that with you."

"I suppose not. This Dom Martini made me nervous. Will you at least tell me what you find out about him?"

"Of course. You and his parents. They may want to tighten security, depending on who this guy is."

"His father already has. When I told him about the visitor, he armed more of the men."

"A sensible response, as long as the men use good judgement."

XX.

Michelle invited Liz for morning coffee a week after their first sex discussion. Before pouring, Michelle reached behind the toaster.

"Have you changed your mind since our last talk?"

"No. I told you I've thought about this for a long time."

"I haven't been able to stop thinking about it. You really planted a seed."

"So you'll do it."

"I'm having trouble getting past the idea that I'll be seducing him."

Liz sighed.

"You've said that after you show him how to do something two or three times, he remembers. Your actions may have to be seductive, but he's a man. He'll appreciate what you've given back to him."

"You may be asking the impossible, Liz. This week, I helped him remember how to kiss. He's really into it. We've done it often. Even that doesn't turn him on."

"I suggest you take the most direct approach. To accomplish this, you can't be shy."

Michelle blushed and glanced at Randy, eating as usual.

"What do you think, Randy? You want me to teach sex education?" He smiled. "You smile whenever I say your name."

"Giving him back his manhood can only make him feel better about himself."

"And you're sure you don't want me to use birth control? I don't want anyone to think I'm after his money."

"I want him to have children. He might never regain his ability to communicate. That shouldn't keep him from becoming a father. There's nothing physically wrong with him. Do you want children?"

"Yes. For as long as I can remember."

"Then Randy will be able to repay your kindness. Let him do this for you."

Michelle bit her lip.

"I'm still not sure. But I'm strongly considering it."

"I won't nag. As a matter of fact, I won't bring it up again. This has to be your decision. Tell me after you've done it."

"Okay. Thanks."

* * *

Kendall always seemed to move with purpose. But Michelle thought he seemed even more determined than usual as he approached the Explorer.

"Morning, Randy. Michelle. Where you two off to?"

"Hi, Kendall. Our first trip to Taos. I'm excited and nervous."

"You have directions to Rachel's place?"

"Yes, sir."

"Good. Agent Lyons just called. The guy who claimed to be Randy's friend is really Dom Barone. He works for the people Randy was investigating when he disappeared. He has an arrest record."

Michelle shuddered.

"I don't understand why they'd send him. Didn't somebody take over that case?"

"Yes. But they never got anywhere. His office has always figured that something he found made him dangerous to them, and they covered it up after they kidnapped him."

"Is he in danger?"

"I think you did a pretty good job of convincing that guy that Randy is no threat to anyone. But keep your eyes open. Obviously, no one can wait for you at the end of the driveway."

"Nowhere to hide."

"Exactly. Liz and I'll make it our policy not to tell anyone when you're going somewhere. You do the same and pass the message on to Rachel. If no one can wait for you to leave or expect you somewhere, you should be pretty safe."

"Sounds good."

Michelle drove to the highway, enjoying the clear fall day. She turned left and set the cruise control, Highway 518 followed the valley until the town of Holman, then switched back into the Sangre de Cristo Mountains.

To the north, she saw snow-covered peaks. Twice, she braked for deer.

"Traffic here is just like home." Randy looked back over his shoulder several times. "We've never gone this far, have we. This country is beautiful. No granite peaks, but still a lot like home."

Just past Rancho de Taos, she picked up Highway 68. She repeatedly checked Rachel's complicated directions, finally reaching a ridge-top road with gentle curves through trees and brush. She slowed, heeding Rachel's warning about their hidden driveway.

A mailbox decorated with dried chilies appeared and she signaled before making the left turn. The paved lane dropped out of the trees and into a bowl, where a large yard surrounded a matching house. Two ponies grazed near a modest shed. Rachel had explained that they owned enough land to support ponies, but the older children had to do their riding at the ranch.

Rachel and her youngest child, Kenny, greeted them. The tension left Randy and he began playing with his nephew. Rachel smiled.

"How'd it go?"

"He kept looking back until we got to Taos. He got tense when I started checking directions."

"He realized that you weren't just going home. He should have known where you were headed. We've lived here since he was in high school."

"I don't understand how his mind works. Until he's reminded, he doesn't remember anyone or anything from before he was kidnapped."

"But he remembered me."

"Not from before. I showed him your picture every day."

"Oh. Let's enjoy the sunshine on the patio. We haven't had time to talk in a week. Has he made any progress?"

"We've been making picture boards. We cut pictures out of magazines and glue them to recipe cards. Beverages. Activities. Lots and lots of foods. He's learning to point at what he wants."

"He's helping you?"

"Yes. Of course, he misses the point. He'll cut out ten pictures of hamburgers and twenty of pie. But he's trying to help. In the process, I discovered that he likes seafood."

"You didn't know that?"

"Elena never served it. Your dad had live lobsters shipped in the other day. Yum."

Rachel chuckled.

"Elena cooks quite a variety of food. Are you enjoying it?"

"Love it. Elena's even given me cooking lessons. It's not like all we ever ate was beef and potatoes. But Mexican food meant tacos from a kit. Seafood was frozen fish sticks or trout from the stream. Chinese would be stir-fried beef and vegetables with sweet and sour sauce. Everything Elena cooks is so much better."

"She's a great cook. I remember her as a little girl, standing on a stool in the kitchen, learning from her mom."

"She said her mom cooked for your parents until she retired."

Rachel just smiled for a moment.

"Elena had such a crush on Randy. I never asked either of

them if he took advantage of that. She never acted like she had a broken heart."

"Oh. I still get a little surprised when someone talks about Randy's ... ah ..."

"Sex life?"

Michelle blushed.

"Yeah. It seems so foreign."

"That's the only thing missing. I mean, of course, he can't talk. But otherwise, he's the same brother he's always been. His humor. The way he won't back down from Susan. His way with the kids. And horses. Has he worked?"

"Your dad told Sam to put him to work if he needed to. He's helped feed cattle and horses. We've herded cattle several times, and we ride fences. I offered to do that, since we ride so much. Randy fixes breaks if he can, or I call in major repairs. I think he likes to feel useful."

"I'm sure of it. Randy's a worker."

∗ ∗ ∗

Liz invited Randy and Michelle to dinner that evening for a report on the day's trip. His parents both expressed satisfaction with the way their son had handled the experience.

"You know, Michelle," Kendall said. "I never thought to ask before. Did you ever take Randy fishing?"

"Yes. We never worry about a fishing license on our own land."

"Fly fishing?"

"No. My brothers tried to teach him, but he wasn't interested enough to watch. He just liked to sit on shore and throw his line out. He caught quite a few."

Kendal chuckled.

"As you've said before, you remind him of what he already knows. I love fly fishing. When he was fourteen, he announced that it was too much like work. He liked going fishing, but he didn't want anything to do with a fly."

"I'm surprised he'll go near the water at all," Liz said.

"Why?" Michelle asked.

Kendall explained.

"When he was five, he fell in a flooding creek. We would have lost him if I hadn't been downstream."

She gazed at Liz.

"So you've nearly lost him twice."

"Yes. You can see why I'm a little overprotective."

Kendall chuckled.

"A lot overprotective. You should have seen her a week later when he wanted to wade in the same creek. He was fearless. I always admired that."

"I didn't. I never took Valium, but Randy made me consider it more than once."

After dinner, Michelle wandered home, deep in thought. She found herself in the bathroom, staring at the shower. Randy tapped her on the shoulder and she looked into his puzzled eyes. She smiled.

"I'm trying to decide if I have the nerve to do this."

She carried a large bath towel to the bedroom and spread it on the bed, feeding his curiosity. Then she locked the front door. When she removed her blouse, he smiled and pulled his sweatshirt off.

"You think you understand. You don't have a clue that I'm planning more than a shower."

But when the time came to abandon subtlety, she lost her nerve, settling for a shower. Her body protested.

"It's wrong. I want it so much. But it's wrong. I'd be seducing you."

She removed the towel, but climbed into bed naked. Randy did nothing to support her decision. Instead, he lay behind her, kissing her neck and caressing her body. The sensations stayed with her all night and throughout the next day.

XXI.

In the evening, she returned to the shower. This time, Michelle ignored her conscience. She watched his face when she set out to seduce him. First surprise. Then pleasure. Then shock.

"That's okay. That's what we wanted to happen."

She led him to the bedroom and pressed him back on the bed. His eyes followed her every hesitant move. Feeling awkward and afraid, she hovered over him. Michelle took a deep breath and forged ahead.

Randy's upper body came off the bed with such force that their heads nearly banged together. Michelle had felt more secure on bucking horses. Every second she expected him to throw them both off the bed. Her fingers dug into his arms, though she doubted he noticed. His eyes stayed closed, his face twisted in agony.

Then he finished. Gasping, he covered his face with his arms. She waited for her heart to stop pounding before lying beside him, with some discomfort. Only his heaving chest moved.

"What have I done? You trusted me and I used you." He began to shake. "Oh, no."

He laughed. Then he pulled his arms back, grinning. She let her breath out.

"You liked it. I thought I'd damaged you for life."

He giggled, hugged her, then giggled again. He sighed and caressed her. The behavior repeated for the next twenty minutes. She finally had to smile.

"At least one of us enjoyed it. The best I can say is, I'm not impressed."

She snuggled into his arms, but before long, he moved, leaning over her. It took a moment for her to recognize that his actions were an attempt to recreate the experience.

"You want to do it *again?*" She groaned. "Well, good luck with that. I won't help you. If you can figure it out, more power to you."

She endured his attention, as awkward as hers had been. To her dismay, he managed to rub his body against hers enough to achieve the desired reaction. When he finished this time, he only giggled once.

He sighed and dozed off, while she tried to sleep. Physical and mental discomfort kept her awake. Her conscience bothered her and she worried because she had not enjoyed the experience. *The shower was so much fun. I thought sex would feel good.*

* * *

His weight woke Michelle. *It's just Randy.* She opened her eyes, surprised. No flashbacks to her sexual assault. Only a matter-of-fact realization that Randy was on her again. This time, he finished faster. She felt only pain.

He doesn't need me to participate, just be present. She bit her lip, fighting tears. She sat up, swung her legs over the side of the bed, and wiped her eyes. He kissed her shoulder and neck.

"Just like everything else. It takes you three times to refine your technique. You just don't understand that I'm not a sex toy. I'm supposed to enjoy this too. I know it's early, but I'm getting up. If I stay in bed, you'll just want more."

In the kitchen, he noticed her mood, and hugged her. But after breakfast, he tried to lead her back to the bedroom. She pulled away.

"No. We're going for a walk."

She slipped on her coat and he followed her outside. A dusting of snow covered the ground and their breath formed clouds of vapor. He cast frequent glances at her. Michelle sighed.

"If I'd waited until you could understand me, I wouldn't have this problem. I wouldn't feel like I've seduced you. And I could tell you that I don't enjoy it, so you could change what you do. Now you just know that something's bothering me, but you don't have a clue what. It wouldn't occur to you that it's sex, because it feels so good to you."

She bit her lip and he wrapped his arm around her waist.

"I know you'd change if you knew. You're so soft-hearted."

They walked to the landing strip in silence. With dread, Michelle headed back, wondering what she could do next rather than return to the house. A visit to Liz seemed a viable excuse. She entered the kitchen of the big house, finding Liz alone-Elena's day off.

"Good morning, you two. I didn't expect to see you out walking so early on a cold morning like this."

"It's still nice compared to back home. And there's no wind today. But some coffee would feel good about now."

"Coming up."

After they removed their coats, Randy pulled Michelle against him.

"No."

She pushed until he released her. Liz froze with the coffee pot poised above a cup.

"You've done it."

"Yes. And he likes it."

Liz smiled.

"I knew he would."

"He's not very good at it."

"He'll get better. Give him time."

"He might wear me out before then. Since he doesn't understand, I plan to teach him that sex stays in the house. Otherwise I'm afraid he might do it anywhere."

"Oh. We don't need that."

Michelle drank coffee, then removed Randy's hand from her belt.

"No! This could take a while. About like telling him not to eat."

"I hadn't considered his lack of inhibitions."

"Me either. I should have waited until he could understand everything we say."

"But we don't know if that will ever happen. You did the right thing."

Michelle stared at her cup, now convinced of the fallacy of Liz's thinking. *But it's too late for that.*

"I have no doubt he'll eventually understand everything."

"I wish I had your confidence. I'm so afraid we'll never have our Randy back. I wish he'd stayed here and worked for one of our papers like we wanted him to. Why did he have to be so independent? And choose such a dangerous profession? If he'd stayed home, none of this would have happened."

* * *

For the next two days, Michelle avoided the house as much as possible, even having lunch and dinner at the big house. But that strategy only served to quicken Randy's pace when they reached the bedroom. She tried to think of something else and ignore the pain. *He's not rough. He just doesn't know I can't get ready as fast as he can. He doesn't mean to hurt me.*

After another early morning session, they walked again. But this time a cold, north wind made walking more miserable than staying inside. Would it be too early to have coffee with Liz? Seeing lust in Randy's eyes, she decided that she did not care.

Elena greeted them in the kitchen.

"People from Wyoming must be tough. I wouldn't walk across the yard in this weather."

"We didn't get far. I didn't think about the wind. At home we don't notice it because of the trees."

Elena poured coffee and studied Randy.

"Tell me to mind my own business if you like. Has Randy remembered what a man likes best?"

Too embarrassed to blush, Michelle shrugged.

"What makes you say that?"

"His eyes. He looks like he would do you right there with me watching."

"He's learned that he can't do it outside of our house."

"Is that why you've spent so much time here?" Michelle nodded. "Is he hurting you?"

"He doesn't mean to. He just doesn't understand."

She could hold the tears no longer. When Randy saw, he stroked her hair, kissed her cheek, and hugged her.

"Oh, Michelle. You're right. He's not like that."

"He's just never satisfied. Sometimes he's ready to go again in a half-hour. I'm not used to this."

"You mean you're not used to his pace?"

"Well. Yes."

"Michelle, were you a virgin?"

"Yes."

"Oh, you poor girl."

"Don't feel sorry for me. I started it. I'm getting what I deserve."

"Why'd you start?"

Michelle wiped her eyes and kissed Randy's hand.

"I think I love him. And Liz ..."

Elena swore in Spanish.

"She talked you into it. It was all her idea, wasn't it?"

"I'd thought about it. She didn't coerce me."

"No. She took advantage of you. She wants that grandchild, doesn't she?"

"Yes. But I understand. She's afraid. She almost lost her son. I should've kept a clear head. I wanted to be talked into it."

"Still, you don't deserve to be abused. That's not what love is. How can he be so tender now, but so heartless when he wants sex?"

"Because I'm crying now. I won't cry then."

"Why not?"

"It wouldn't be fair. I'd be manipulating him."

"So manipulate him. You have to take care of yourself."

"It would be cruel."

"If you keep letting him hurt you, you'll end up hating him. Which is worse?" When Michelle said nothing, she continued. "Look at him. There's no lust now. If he could understand what you say, you'd tell him he's hurting you. Right?"

"Yes."

"He understands tears. Speak to him in a language he understands."

Elena worked around the kitchen, giving her time to think. Randy continued to comfort her. Finally, Michelle sighed.

"He'll get frustrated."

"He'll live. If he gets too hard to handle, send him to me." She grinned at Michelle's shocked expression. "I've always wondered what it would be like. He was too much of a gentleman to take advantage of me, no matter how much I wanted it."

"Someone told me you used to have a crush on him."

"Still do. He was my first kiss. I would have done anything for him. But he said he'd just be using me. He couldn't do it. I figured he didn't think I was good enough and I told him so. He was eighteen and he had a lot of girls then." Elena smiled at the memory. "He said he didn't care about them. He cared about me. Since then, he's treated me like his little sister."

"He doesn't want to hurt me."

"No. But you have to find a way to let him know he's hurting you. As early in foreplay as you can."

"Foreplay? He doesn't need it."

"Oh. Then as soon as he shows any interest. Do it for both of you."

"I will. Thanks for helping me see that I have options."

"No problem. If you need to talk, come to me. Mrs. Liz will support you if it means helping Randy. But she will always choose what's best for him, even if it's not good for you."

"I should have seen that."

XXII.

Randy surprised Michelle by not accosting her as soon as they returned to the house. He watched her with concern while she worked for a half-hour.

He's not insensitive. He knows I was upset about something.

When he finally approached her, he just held her for a moment before he began unbuttoning her blouse. Crying came easily. She had held it in for too long. He stood back, then just hugged her.

Three more times that day, she cried when he wanted sex. He held her, showing no sign of frustration, only confusion. At bedtime, he tried again with the same result. He sat up, staring at her.

"I'm sorry. I know you don't understand. It's the only way I can get a break from you. I just need a couple days off."

He snuggled up to her and held her until she fell asleep.

Michelle refused him all the next day, then prepared herself to accept him the following morning. But her tears had made him cautious. He waited until after breakfast. When he began undressing her, she would not let the tears come. She led him to the bedroom and he finished removing her clothes.

He stripped, grinning, while she lay down. He nearly jumped

on the bed with her. Michelle bit her lip, ready to endure. Randy lowered himself, stopped, then frowned. He sat back, gazing at her, his interest gone.

Tears ran down her cheeks. He sighed and lay beside her, wiping the tears away. His expression asked, "What's wrong?"

"I'm sorry, Randy. I just don't enjoy it. It hurts. I thought it would feel good."

He sighed again. Then he began stroking all of her favorite places. It took a few minutes for the pleasure to penetrate. Michelle gasped, then moaned, repeatedly. He smiled, showing no sign of arousal himself. She finally stopped him.

"I don't think you see any connection between this and sex. Let's make the connection."

She encouraged him to continue touching her, then wrapped her arms around him and began kissing his neck. Still nothing. He brushed the small of her back, and she momentarily forgot her goal. With her mind refocused, she began stoking him. He caught his breath.

When he drew back to study her, she smiled and he laughed.

"Now you get it."

She pulled him close for a long kiss, which evolved into her first enjoyable sexual experience. They both finished out of breath and smiling. She caressed his damp body, relief flooding her until she had to fight tears again. His smile faded and she laughed to reassure him.

"It was great. Really. These are happy tears."

He seemed skeptical. Lavish attention finally convinced him. He sighed, contented this time. She hugged him.

"I'll still have to tell you 'no' sometimes. Until I get used to how often you can do this. But if you do it just like you did this morning, we'll get along fine."

✳ ✳ ✳

A week later, Michelle and Randy stopped at the main house for coffee after their morning walk. Elena smiled.

"Haven't seen much of you the past week. Are things going better over there?"

Michelle returned the smile as she sat by the kitchen island. "Much."

"Why, Michelle, you look satisfied."

"Yes. I'd have to say that. He figured it out."

"Good. I was really worried about you. You think he has any idea that he could be making a baby?"

"Not a clue."

"The next few months could get very interesting."

"Tell me about it. I've always wanted to have kids, but it's a little scary."

"He's so good with kids."

"Good morning, everyone," Liz said from the doorway. She stopped to kiss Randy's cheek, then cast a stern glance from Michelle to Elena. "Michelle, have you broadcast this to anyone else?"

Michelle bristled.

"I didn't tell Elena. She could see it in his eyes. Haven't you noticed?"

"No."

"Well, he's insatiable. If you pay attention, in about a half-hour, he'll look like he's ready to do it right here on the kitchen counter."

"Oh, dear. It won't do for everyone to know about this. Can't you do anything to discourage him?"

Michelle laughed a humorless laugh.

"Any suggestions?"

"Ah, no." Liz drank the coffee Elena had poured. "I guess we'll just have to deal with it. Be sure he's satisfied before you leave home." Michelle said nothing. "Has his performance improved?"

"Yes."

"I knew it would."

"Yeah. We're going to Taos tomorrow."

"Is that smart? He'll have to go without for quite a while."

"I need to get away. I've made allowances for his sex drive long enough. He'll have to make allowances for my plans tomorrow. It'll be good for him."

* * *

Randy studied Michelle from the passenger seat, the same way he had for the past half-hour. She smirked.

"I confused the heck out of you. I not only gave you your wake up sex, but I insisted on after-breakfast sex too. What's going on?" He yawned. "You're right. I was trying to wear you out."

He leaned back and dozed during part of the trip. Once again, they found Rachel and Kenny in the yard. Randy played with his nephew while Michelle helped put out Thanksgiving decorations. Rachel paused to watch her brother.

"What are you staring at?" Michelle asked.

"Is he doing what Kenny asks him to?"

Michelle studied Randy for a moment.

"Yes. With qualifications. Kenny says up and raises his arms. He got on the swing and asked Randy to push him. Randy understands from context. And he recognizes a lot of words."

"You think that's all it is?"

"I *think* so. I know he's getting better. But I don't think he can understand instructions."

"Couldn't we make up some kind of test?"

"Well. How about colors? He's never been able to grasp colors. If I showed him a blue towel, then asked him to pick out blue again, he'd pick a red towel rather than a blue ball."

"Let's try it. We'll use crayons. Kenny, let's go in."

"Aw, Mom!"

"You can play a game with Uncle Randy."

"What kind of game?"

"We'll quiz him on his colors."

"Doesn't he know them?"

"He forgot them when the bad thing happened to him."

"Oh."

They shed their coats.

"Bring your crayons to the kitchen. I'll make hot chocolate."

Rachel had her back turned when Randy pulled Michelle against him and she pushed him away. He sighed, but sat beside her at the table. Kenny sat on Randy's lap, effectively distracting him. Michelle sorted through the crayons, choosing common colors. She instructed Kenny.

"Ask Randy to pick out colors."

"Okay. Uncle Randy, pick the blue color."

"He doesn't understand a lot of words. Just say the name of the color."

"Okay. Blue." He waited, then guided Randy's hand to the blue crayon. Randy smiled. "Green." Again he guided Randy's hand. "Red."

This time he did not help. Randy's hand moved slowly to the red crayon. Rachel squealed, while Michelle remained cautious. Kenny smiled.

"Right! Black." Randy hesitated, then pointed at the brown crayon. "Close. I used to get those mixed up too. That's brown." He moved Randy's hand between the brown and black crayon. "Brown. Black. Brown. Black. See."

Randy smiled.

"Purple." Randy found the right one. Kenny quizzed him on the ten colors on the table and he made no more mistakes. "Good job. He knows his colors, Mom. Why you crying?"

"Oh, honey, that's a big step for Uncle Randy. It means his head is working better."

"His head works okay. It's just his mouth that's broke."

Rachel laughed and wiped her tears.

"Well, it's a little more complicated than that."

Randy looked from Michelle to Rachel, finding the tears and smiles confusing. Michelle kissed his cheek.

"Sometimes women cry when they're happy." She sighed. "I'll sure be glad when you can understand everything I say."

"He's a man," Rachel said. "That'll never happen."

XXIII.

"Three inches," Michelle said to her mother.

"Three inches? And that qualifies as a blizzard?"

"Yeah. The weather was nasty. Cold and windy, and you couldn't see a hundred yards. But then it warmed up. There's still snow under the trees, or where it drifted in behind something. But the rest of the ground's bare. You don't need pack boots or snow shoes. I just wear insulated hiking boots."

"Any chance you can come home for Christmas?"

"I'd like to. But Randy gets anxious if he's away from me more than a few minutes."

"You still think he can be weaned in a year?"

Michelle chuckled.

"I think so. He recognizes a lot of words. He can pick out colors, and what he wants to eat or drink. Imagine what he'll be able to do nine months from now."

"Have they found the other person who kidnapped him?"

"No. No progress there."

"Okay. We won't talk about that. Tell me good news. What's your next step?"

"That's a big one. Mc Donald's. We're going to see Rachel again tomorrow."

"You're taking him inside a restaurant?"

"Yeah. Mid-afternoon. Before school's out."

"Good luck."

* * *

Michelle drove to Taos on a sunny, snow-melting morning, feeling especially good when she heard another blizzard forecast for the states north of New Mexico.

By the time they left Rachel's place for the restaurant, the day had become gray, though they did not need to zip their coats.

When they reached the Mc Donald's, Randy refused to enter. Michelle smiled.

"Well, we're going in."

They left him alone outside. He grimaced and shifted from one foot to the other. She watched him, trying not to show her own anxiety.

He rushed through the doors and wrapped his arms around her. She rubbed his back.

"I know it wasn't easy. But you'll like this place. You can eat all you want."

"Just don't deplete my trust fund," Rachel said.

Randy inhaled and looked over Michelle's shoulder toward the counter. She took his hand and led him to a female employee.

"Can we see a picture menu?"

Michelle smiled, then laughed, as he selected enough items to feed her all day. After Kenny made up his mind, Rachel shelled out the sizable cost of their meal. She and Michelle carried trays to a deserted corner of the restaurant.

Randy wolfed his food, ignoring a female employee who cleaned tables nearby. But when a young man entered the area with a mop, he stopped eating. Michelle rested her hand on his forearm, feeling his muscles tighten.

"Excuse me. Strangers make him nervous. Could you avoid this spot until we finish?"

He shrugged and moved away. Randy attacked his food again.

She picked at her fries and noticed papers scurry across the parking lot. Shrubs bent and flags cracked, pointing straight south.

"That's a nasty north wind," Rachel said.

"We'd better head home as soon as we drop you off."

"Let's listen to a forecast first. I don't want you traveling on bad roads."

"It's less than an hour. We'll be home before dark."

"Just humor me."

Michelle nodded, hoping for a good forecast. Randy would expect sex even if they had to stay overnight. She wondered how long she could keep Rachel and her family from noticing his advances.

They left the building and ran for the Explorer.

"Oh, Lord!" Rachel said. "Can you believe how cold it's gotten?"

Michelle tuned in a local radio station before she left the parking lot. The forecast came on as the first raindrops struck the windshield. Her heart sank when she heard the travel advisory for freezing rain.

"Oh, no."

"You'll just stay with us tonight. I'll call Mom."

Michelle considered ways she could talk herself out of Taos. But when ice began forming on her windshield, she discarded the idea. She had more sense than to drive on icy mountain roads. She parked her vehicle in Rachel's driveway.

"I think Randy needs some space before Darren and the kids get home."

"I hadn't thought of that. The guest bedroom's downstairs. I'll keep Kenny busy. You can have the whole floor to yourselves."

"Thanks."

When they entered the bedroom, Michelle locked the door and pulled off her crew neck sweater. He stripped in the time it took her to remove her shoes.

"You poor guy. No sex for almost seven hours. How *did* you survive?"

He finished undressing her and pushed her back on the bed, rushing. She shoved with both hands and a glare. He proceeded at a slower pace. She had to concentrate to keep from screaming, not wanting to explain that to Rachel.

They just lay together until daylight faded. She stretched and sat up.

"We'd better get dressed. Time to be sociable."

* * *

The kids kept Randy occupied during the evening, discovering that he could play checkers, Operation, and Connect Four. They kept switching games when he beat them.

"I wonder if he can still play chess," Darren said.

Rachel laughed.

"You hated playing chess with him."

"Because he always whipped me. Maybe now I can beat him."

"If you want to challenge him, get out the chess set. Okay, kids. Bedtime."

Randy jumped on the love seat beside Michelle and wrapped his arms around her. She doubted that he could concentrate on another game.

"I think your challenge will have to wait. This one seems to be ready for bed."

Darren grinned.

"Just as well. I'd feel even more humiliated if he could still beat me in his condition."

"I'll get you those clothes," Rachel said.

She brought T-shirts and sweat pants for both of them. Michelle made a mental note to give them a slept in look as she and Randy descended the stairs.

Darren and Rachel elected to call it an early evening as well. Rachel turned back the bed.

"What's that noise?"

Darren stopped brushing his teeth to listen, then spoke around his toothbrush.

"Sounds like a squeaking bed."

"Why ...?" Rachel scowled. "Only one thing makes a bed squeak like that."

Darren removed his toothbrush.

"Oh, come on Rachel. A bed sounds like that when the kids jump on it."

"She's not jumping on *the bed*. She's taking advantage of my little brother."

"Rachel. He's probably having the time of his life."

"He has the mind of a child. She seduced him."

"Don't jump to conclusions. Wait till you hear her side of it."

"Fine. Let's go."

"Now? Can't it wait until morning?"

"You think I can sleep, knowing what she's doing to him."

Darren sighed at her departing back and grabbed his robe. By the time he reached the stairs, she was pounding on the guest room door.

"Michelle, come out here. I know what you're doing."

"Keep your voice down. You want the kids in on this conversation?"

Rachel paced until Michelle, wearing a long T-shirt and a horrified expression, opened the door just far enough to leave the room. Rachel stopped pacing.

"How could you? We trusted you. Randy trusts you."

Michelle took a deep breath.

"I did it with your mom's blessing."

"What?"

"Rachel," Darren said. "Keep your voice down."

"I don't believe it. You seduced my brother."

Michelle nodded.

"Yes, I did. At your mother's suggestion."

Darren stroked Rachel's hair.

"Think about it, Rachel. Your parents were devastated when

they thought he died childless. Your mom saw a chance to make sure that doesn't happen. What Michelle says is true to form."

Rachel sank to the nearest chair.

"You're right. Mom acts out of fear." She gazed at Michelle. "So you're not practicing safe sex."

"Darren's right. She wants him to be a father."

"And you let her talk you into this?" Randy, au naturel, opened the bedroom door and wrapped his arms around Michelle, grinning. Rachel blushed and averted her eyes. "Is he always so shy?"

"He'll undress anywhere he feels comfortable."

"That's new. I haven't seen so much of him since he was a toddler."

Darren patted her back.

"I told you he's having the time of his life. He doesn't have to work and he gets as much sex as he wants."

Rachel gazed at her brother.

"Do you think he knows that he could be making a baby?"

Michelle stroked his arm.

"I don't think so."

"Why are you doing this?"

"Because I love him. I'll admit it may have clouded my judgement."

Rachel nodded.

"That makes sense. I didn't think that you were after his money. Mom wouldn't have tried to talk you into this if you were."

"Can we go to bed now?" Darren asked.

"Go on. I'll be along in a minute." She waited until he left. "Who knows about this?"

"Your mom has been pretty secretive about it. She didn't want me to tell anybody. Elena figured it out. I've taught him that we only do this in the house. Until today, that worked."

"Do you think it will be a problem, now that he knows he can have sex anywhere?"

"No. I think he understands that you already know."

"Are you pregnant?"

"Not as of last week. Try explaining that to a man who can perform up to five times a day."

Rachel covered a grin.

"Especially when he can't understand what you say. How did he take that?"

"Oh, he was in a mood all four days. He may understand the word 'no,' but he doesn't like it."

"Randy, you're living up to your name."

XXIV.

Michelle demonstrated Randy's new understanding of colors to Dr. Lopez. When she finished all of his tests, Michelle smiled and thanked him. Randy caressed her arm.

Dr. Lopez nodded.

"He's made excellent progress. He seems to be well on his way to becoming a fully functioning adult. I'll continue to see him monthly until we can have a two-way communication. However, I want you to contact me if he begins to give you problems."

"I don't see that happening."

"Perhaps you're too close to see the change. He's treating you differently. Rather than acting like your guardian, he's acting like a man."

Michelle laughed.

"What do you mean?"

"The way he touches you has changed. Instead of hugs, he is very tender. Be watchful for sexual advances."

"Oh. Randy understands when I tell him 'no.' I'm not concerned."

"Don't take a nonchalant attitude. Neither of you needs to have a bad experience. If he begins making advances, we can put him on medication to suppress his urges."

Michelle considered commenting on how that contradicted the goal of having him become a fully functioning adult. But she decided that a change of subject might prove more prudent.

"I'll keep my eyes open. Let me tell you about our trip to Mc Donald's."

Michelle gave her the details of the experience, even mentioning the overnight stay. Dr. Lopez nodded several times.

"Did he respond any differently under those conditions?"

"Not at all. He seems contented as long as I'm with him."

"He's very attached to you. As his understanding increases, I'll expect you to spend time away from him. You both need that."

"Of course. That makes perfect sense. But I don't think it'll be easy for either of us."

* * *

Michelle held her hand over the sink to avoid bleeding on the floor. She applied pressure to the cut.

"Randy!"

He hurried from the bedroom.

"Hand me that towel."

When he did, she used it to apply pressure and stem the blood flow.

"Get the first aid kit out of the bathroom."

He retrieved it, opened the kit, and pulled out gauze pads, tape, and antiseptic. She waited until he had everything prepared before removing the towel. She winced when he disinfected the wound, then held the padding in place until he taped it. The blood did not soak through the gauze.

"Good. I was afraid I'd need stitches. Thanks. Would you throw that broken glass away? Just don't cut yourself like I did."

She watched him place it in the trash, along with the empty bandage wrappers. She only realized what had happened when he closed the first aid kit.

"You just did everything I told you to."

He grinned.

"You understand everything I say."

He wrapped his arms around her.

"But you can't answer me. I have to test this theory. Pick me up."

He obeyed.

"Put me down."

He laughed as he complied. She began to cry.

"Oh, Randy. This is huge."

She wrapped her arms around him, completely forgetting the bandaged hand. He stroked her hair while she sobbed. Finally, he pushed her back, revealing his bewildered expression.

"These are happy tears. Let's go tell your mom."

He sighed, but helped her put her coat on before grabbing his. When they stepped off the porch, he scooped her up and carried her to the other house. Michelle laughed. He opened the door without dropping her and carried her into the kitchen.

Liz had just added vegetables to a kettle containing a beef roast. She set the cover in place. Elena's day off.

"What are you two so giddy about?"

"Randy, put me down and go hug your mom."

He did exactly as she said. It took Liz a moment to recognize the significance of that event. She covered her mouth.

"Oh-h. He ... understands."

"Everything I say. I think."

"I think I'm going to cry."

"Then I won't be alone. I can't stop bawling."

"What happened to your hand?"

"I cut it. He did everything I asked him to."

Randy extracted himself from his mother's arms and returned to Michelle. He wiped her tears and she laughed.

"I know. This is ridiculous. But I just can't stop."

Liz stared at her.

"Are you pregnant?"

Michelle blinked. She felt Randy's muscles tighten.

"Well, that got his attention. I don't know. I'm a few days late, but that doesn't really mean much with me."

"I have a home pregnancy test. I'll get it."

Michelle gazed up at Randy's scowl.

"Your mother even has a home pregnancy test ready for the occasion."

His scowl deepened. Liz returned, waving the box.

"Here you are. This is so exciting."

"Randy would disagree with you."

Liz met his glare with an innocent look. Then she shook her finger at him.

"Don't take that attitude with me, young man. Granted, you had no idea what you were doing when Michelle got you started. But don't try to tell me that you haven't known for a while what could happen."

Randy looked only a little less indignant. He waved Michelle toward the bathroom and she shuffled in that direction.

"Don't expect me soon. I've never done this before. I have to read the instructions."

Randy almost succeeded in fighting back a smile. Liz said nothing, trying to stay busy while they waited. A few minutes later, Michelle returned, appearing slightly dazed. He threw up his hands and turned his glare on a delighted Liz again. She hugged Michelle.

"Oh, Michelle. I'm so happy."

"Well, that makes one of us."

"But you wanted this baby."

"I know. Be careful what you wish for. And now he's mad."

"Oh, don't worry about him. He'll get over it. Randy, if you have to be mad, be mad at me. I had to talk her into it. And this never would have happened if you had married that Reynolds girl like I wanted you to."

He raised his eyebrows. Michelle frowned.

"Who?"

"Oh, that's ancient history. He dated her his first year in college. She had plenty of money. She wasn't after his."

"I'm still not after his money. Just don't forget that."

"I won't. I know you have Randy's best interest at heart."

Randy made a sound that could only signal frustration and left the house. Michelle's eyes overflowed again.

"He hates me."

"Oh, no, Michelle. He's just like any man who wasn't expecting this news. They get over it eventually. He loves kids. He'll look forward to it once he gets used to the idea."

"He'll forgive me?"

"You don't need to be forgiven. You did this for him. He'll see that."

"Okay. What should I do now? I suppose I should see a doctor."

"Before long. But there's no rush. Stay active, but don't try anything new. Keep taking your vitamins and drinking your orange juice. Rest when you need to. And let me break the news to the rest of the family. I'll just give Kendall one piece of good news at a time. Tonight, I'll tell him that Randy can understand."

"Okay. I think I need to rest now. I'll see you later."

✳ ✳ ✳

Michelle noticed Randy on the fence by the horses when she returned to their house. She resisted the urge to go to him. Instead she lay down for a nap.

When she opened her eyes, she found Randy sitting on a chair, frowning at her. She studied him for a moment.

"I see you're still mad at me."

He ran his hands through his hair.

"I don't blame you. I seduced you, plain and simple. I'm not proud of it ..."

He closed the distance between them and touched his fingers to her lips. Michelle gazed at him, trying to understand.

"You are mad at me, aren't you?"

He kissed her, perhaps longer than he ever had. She caught her breath.

"Okay. So you're not mad at me. But you're upset. Maybe your mom's right. You're just shocked to get this news."

He covered his ears and glared.

"You don't want to talk about your mom. But you do need a while to get used to the idea of this baby. So do I."

He hugged her.

"I love you, Randy. I'm sorry I did this to you."

He kissed her and began unbuttoning her blouse. She lay back and watched him, now seeing everything he did as an attempt to communicate. She cooperated, then waited while he undressed. Before anything else, he caressed her breasts. She caught her breath and smiled at his grin.

"You understand everything, don't you. I could never convince you that I wouldn't slap your hand again."

He made love to her very, very slowly. Finally, gasping for air, she begged him to finish. After he did, he dropped to the bed beside her and she snuggled into his arms. They lay together for several minutes.

"Are you trying to say that you're not sorry that I seduced you?"

He kissed her on the nose.

"I'll take that as a yes."

XXV.

Kendall could not contain his exuberance at being able to communicate with his son. Michelle reminded him to watch Randy's body language, his only way to reply. But Randy had to underline that point by walking out on him in mid-sentence. After that, Kendall paid attention.

Michelle waited for Kendall's reaction to the baby. But a week passed without a word. She began to wonder why Liz delayed. Perhaps Kendall would not like the news any more than Randy had.

Eight days after she took the pregnancy test, Kendall burst in on Michelle and Randy while they drank their morning coffee.

"How could you? How could you betray our trust like this? How could you take advantage of our son?"

Michelle just stared for a minute.

"Is that what she told you?"

"Of course, she told me. You won't get away with this!"

Randy leaped to his feet and let his physical presence force his father away from Michelle. Then he stormed out of the house.

Michelle wished that he had stayed. But she had an insurance policy.

"Wait here."

"Don't tell me what to do. You ..."

But Michelle had left the room. Kendall fumed for a moment. She returned just before Randy burst in, dragging Liz by the wrist. Kendall looked from one to the other, his anger tempered.

Liz cringed when Randy shook his fist at her.

"Liz?" Kendall said. "Why's Randy so mad at you?"

"Oh-h."

Michelle held up her digital recorder.

"Tell him, Liz. Or should I just play this? I'm not quite as trusting as you thought."

The color drained from Liz's face and a tear rolled down her cheek.

"I'm sorry. Kendall, it was all my idea. I had to talk Michelle into this. I convinced her that Randy needed to be a father."

Kendall sank to a chair.

"Ah, Liz. He just needed time. If you had just given him time, he could have made the decision himself. You betrayed your own son."

"I just wanted what was best for him."

"You saw a way to finally get what you wanted. You manipulated him. And Michelle. You set up your own little grandchild breeding program."

"You make me sound heartless. I did it because I love him."

"Yes, I suppose you did. That doesn't excuse you." He turned toward Michelle. "And this doesn't excuse you. She's a distraught mother. What's your excuse?"

Randy waved his arms in a gesture that could only mean 'Enough!' Kendall understood.

"You can excuse her for this?"

Randy wrapped his arms around Michelle and she answered for him.

"The day we found out about the baby, he made it clear that

he's not mad at me. He's not thrilled about becoming a father, but he really enjoyed the process."

Randy grinned and Kendall fought a smile.

"Okay. If you enjoyed 'the process' so much, then you deserve the consequences. I expect you to be a good father."

Randy caressed Michelle's belly and his eyes spoke to her. She wiped tears away.

"He's happy."

"Anybody can see that. I expect you to be a good mother too."

"Oh, I will. I promise."

"Liz, we have more to discuss. But we can do it at home."

* * *

Michelle could forgive Liz, but she no longer trusted her. Randy seemed unwilling to even forgive her. If he had been capable of speech, he would not have been speaking to her. The strain in their relationship made ranch life uncomfortable. Michelle compensated with more frequent trips to Taos.

Rachel's support meant a lot to both of them. She helped Michelle choose a doctor and took her to her first appointment. They waited together in an exam room. Michelle fidgeted.

"Do you think Randy's okay?"

"He's fine. He chose to stay with Darren. He knew he couldn't handle this."

"He would have felt claustrophobic. He'd be having an anxiety attack by now."

"Right. Just because he understands, doesn't mean he can handle everything that comes his way. He still has some pretty bad experiences to deal with."

"We'll go right back to your place when we get done."

"No. We're going shopping. And maybe I'll take you out to coffee after that."

"Shopping? I don't have time to go shopping."

"Where do you have to be in such a hurry?"

"I need to get back to Randy."

"No, you don't. We'll call and let him know that everything's fine. Then we'll go shopping. You're having separation anxiety. You and Randy *need* to spend time apart."

"Well. I suppose."

"You believe he'll get better, don't you."

"Yes."

"That means he'll eventually go back to work. You have to get used to being separated."

Michelle sighed.

"Am I clingy?"

"No. You're overprotective. You need to let him be an adult."

"Am I just like your mother?"

Rachel laughed.

"You're in danger of becoming that."

"Okay. I'll go shopping."

"Good. I'll bet you haven't been shopping since he came into your life."

"If you don't count the times we sat in the pickup while my mom shopped."

"That's not shopping. You need maternity clothes. Have you told your parents?"

"No. How do I tell them that I've made a shambles of everything I believe? How do I tell them that I chose to seduce Randy?"

"You'll have to sooner or later."

"Later."

"Just tell them before the baby comes. They'll take it better."

"Okay. I'll plan on that."

✳ ✳ ✳

Randy wrapped his arms around Michelle's naked body, caressing her slightly bulging belly. She leaned her head back against him.

"I'm putting on too much weight."

He kissed her neck.

"Thanks. I suppose we should get dressed. We don't want to be late for your parents' anniversary party. I'm sure not looking forward to seeing Susan."

Randy laughed and reached for his jeans. He chose a western shirt and bolo tie, while she wore maternity pants and a loose shirt. She smiled.

"You sure dress a lot better since you started picking your own clothes. I picked yours like I pick mine. Easy."

He took her hand, raised it above her head, and nudged her into a pirouette. Then he kissed the ends of his fingers in a gesture of approval. She blushed.

"You're very fluent in body language."

He wrapped his arm around her and they hurried to the other house without coats. When they reached the kitchen, he released her. They joined the rest of the family in the livingroom. Everyone waited for Susan's reaction.

She put down her drink and took another drag on her cigarette, blowing a smoke ring like a dark-haired dragon.

"My. My. Nursemaid, you've really porked out on all this free food. What have you put on, twenty pounds?"

Michelle suddenly wanted to rub salt into a wound and knew how to do it. She smiled.

"You're wrong. I'm not fat. I'm pregnant."

Randy laughed, while Susan's jaw tightened and her face turned red. Rachel hid a smile, but the rest of the family just waited. Susan turned to her parents.

"Are you going to let her get away with this? She's trying to get her paws on your money."

Liz folded her hands in her lap.

"It was my idea."

Susan crushed out her cigarette with such force that she spilled the contents of the ashtray.

"You're so intent on getting that *precious* Mc Kay grandchild that you put your mindless wonder out to stud."

That brought another laugh from Randy. She glared at him. Kendall responded.

"He's not quite so mindless as you think. He's happy about becoming a father. And, yes, we welcome another grandchild."

"Not *another* grandchild. *The* grandchild. The heir. You treat the rest of your grandchildren like dirt. Dennis. Trevor. We're leaving. And we're never coming back."

As she stalked out, Randy waved to her departing back, still laughing. Dennis slammed the door behind them. Rachel quit hiding her grin.

"Was that a promise? I took that as a promise."

"I hope so," Michelle said.

Liz sighed.

"It's sad, but unfortunately, so do I."

"And you don't treat your other grandchildren like dirt," Rachel said.

"We know. There's just no pleasing her. She's always been jealous of Randy and she always will be."

"Speaking of Randy. You dog, you were gloating."

He placed his hand on his chest and raised his eyebrows.

"Yes, you. You just loved rubbing it in."

He chuckled and wrapped his arms around Michelle. After a kiss, she spoke.

"I'm sorry. When she gave me that opening, I just couldn't resist. I got tired of her treating me like a servant."

"It's okay," Kendall said. "We've spent too many years trying to appease her. It's time we quit making allowances. This celebration will be more fun without her."

XXVI.

"Living with you is like a never ending game of charades," Michelle said, smiling. "I'm getting pretty good at it. It seems like you should be able to nod your head. Let's try it."

Randy's brow furrowed. She touched his chin.

"Just try it. Move your head up and down."

He did.

"Great! I knew you could do it. Now side to side."

He shook his head negatively.

"Wonderful! Now I'll ask you a real easy question. You try to answer. Do you like sex?"

His grin faded into a frown. His jaw tightened and he finally began shaking. She hugged him.

"Relax. Relax. You tried. There's just something in your brain that won't work. It'll come just like your understanding did. We need to give it more time."

He sighed and buried his face in her hair. When he quivered, she suspected that he was crying. She rubbed his back.

"It's okay. Don't let it get you down."

She held him for as long as he wanted. He finally pulled away, wiped his eyes, and shuffled to the bedroom. Michelle bit her lip, deciding to let him deal with this.

* * *

Three days later, Dr. Lopez diagnosed clinical depression.

"Until now, he didn't realize what he had lost. With understanding comes frustration. He's an intelligent man with no way of expressing himself."

"I sent him into depression by insisting that he try to communicate."

"You were just doing what you've done all along. You had no reason to change your approach. Has he also lost interest in sex?"

Michelle blushed. Dr. Lopez had been less than pleased when Liz told her about the pregnancy. She had accused both Michelle and Liz of plotting a rape. Randy silenced her by demonstrating how much he enjoyed Michelle's company. He had made all three women blush.

"Yes."

"Given his enthusiasm, that's significant. I'll see him again next week. I'll ask the psychiatrist on our staff to prescribe medication."

"What can I do until then?"

"Encourage him to resume his usual activities. Is he eating?"

"Yes. But not like Randy. Since I've known him, he's devoured his food. He's not eating as much, or as fast."

Dr. Lopez nodded.

"Don't be discouraged if he resists your urging. Depression is like that. If it worsens, call me immediately."

After Dr. Lopez departed, Michelle stroked Randy's hair. He had not moved from the sofa in nearly two hours.

"Let's go."

She pulled on his hand. After staring at her for a moment, he yielded, rising like an old man. She tugged him along to the kitchen and handed him a jacket. When he had that on, she gave him his hiking boots, and pulled on one of his sweatshirts. She could no longer fasten her jacket.

"Let's go. Come on. It's a beautiful day for a walk."

He only dragged his feet until they left the porch. Although he still seemed depressed, he kept up with her. Exercise would do them both good.

"I can't let myself get soft. Having a baby is hard enough if you're in good shape."

She stopped at the horse pasture, hoping to peak his interest. Randy scratched the horses without enthusiasm. Continuing their stroll, Michelle paused by anything that she thought might gain his attention. Nothing did.

They walked all the way to the airplane hanger. She poked around the spacious building, circling an old Jeep, the twin-engine plane, and a single engine plane.

Randy barely looked at her. She sighed and walked around the building into the scrub evergreens, their scent reminding her of home. A more adventurous return route might help him.

Within a half-mile, she decided that the more adventurous route should be left for the downhill part of their hike. She worked her way back toward the road, accepting Randy's help when he offered it. Once on the road, she stopped to rest, leaning on him. The sound of a vehicle coming from the ranch made them move to the shoulder.

Liz stopped her Yukon beside them.

"I was getting worried. You're not usually gone this long."

"We walked all the way to the hanger. Exercise can help him feel better."

"You look tired. Would you like a ride back?"

"Thanks, no. I'll take a nap when we get home."

"Are you sure? You don't need to overdo it."

"I'm fine. A little tired, but not exhausted."

"Okay. If you're sure."

Liz turned around in the road and they resumed their hike. When they reached the house, Michelle felt close to exhausted. Randy helped her remove the sweatshirt. She sat to take off her boots, but did not move. He unlaced them for her.

"Thanks. I'm going to take a nap now. Want to join me?"

He guided her to the bedroom.

* * *

The next day, Michelle planned a shorter walk. Randy again kept up with her, but showed no interest in anything. When they returned to the house, she had enough energy for the second phase of her plan. After they had their outerwear and boots off, she led him to the bathroom and unbuttoned his shirt.

He studied her.

"I know it's not the usual time of day for a shower, but we didn't have one yesterday. We need it."

They finished undressing and slid into the shower. After she washed his back, she turned and he reciprocated. Then he began a more thorough washing, dwelling on her bulging belly. She rested her hands on his.

"Admiring your handiwork?"

He sighed. After a moment, he resumed lathering her body, producing a series of moans. He wrapped his arms around her and sighed again. Michelle gave her pulse time to subside before facing him. She took the soap from him and sudsed his chest before laying it aside.

"How's this for subtle?"

He watched her hand slide down from his chest, disinterested. She persisted. He met her gaze and the corner of his mouth flickered up. His eyes brightened and he pulled her into a very long kiss. She only moved her hands to his shoulders when she felt the effect of her foreplay.

Randy turned off the shower, then dried both of them before they returned to the bedroom. He made love to her in the gentle way that he had adopted as her pregnancy progressed. When they finished, he held her, caressing her belly.

Michelle sighed.

"I hope you feel better. I certainly do.

He smiled.

"I'm sorry I sent you into that depression."

He smiled and kissed her nose.

"You're so sweet. I won't push you so hard anymore."

He held her chin and gazed at her.

"I know. I'll try not to be so hard on myself. I was just trying to help."

He smiled and replaced his hand on her belly. The baby kicked and he jerked to attention, now grinning.

"Pretty neat, huh."

He gave her a very long kiss that progressed to another round of making love.

* * *

Michelle placed her cake in the oven and set the timer, then checked on Randy. She found him on the sofa with one of his Tony Hillerman novels. A paperback. The autographed hard covers were strictly collectors' items.

He smiled at her before returning his attention to the book. He turned a page.

"Are you reading?"

He grinned. Michelle smiled.

"Progress." She watched until he turned another page. "That gives me an idea. I'll get back to you."

She retrieved the box of supplies she had used to make flash cards for Randy. She selected blank cards, writing a word on each. When the timer sounded, she had quite a collection. Randy wandered from the livingroom, interested in the cake.

"Perfect timing. I'll explain this to you. Over here I have people—I, Michelle, Mom, Dad, etc. This bunch is actions—walk, stand, sit, sleep. You get the picture. These are things. Chair, table, kitchen, barn. And this bunch is feelings. Happy, sad, mad, love. It won't be proper English, but I thought you could try to make sentences."

Randy studied the cards.

"I'll ask you a question, see if you can form an answer. Don't push yourself too hard. If it doesn't come, that's okay. What were you doing in the living room?"

His brow furrowed. Finally, he selected the "I." She held her breath. He added "read," then finished with "book." She fought tears. He had not finished. He placed "sit" in the middle and added "sofa."

"Oh, Randy."

He continued. He placed "Michelle" at the end and moved "love" to the middle. He kissed her tear-stained cheeks.

"Oh, Randy. I love you, too."

XXVII.

"It's inconvenient," Michelle said to Rachel while they watched Randy playing with Kenny in Rachel's yard. "But it lets him communicate."

"Has he said anything profound?"

Michelle smiled.

"He loves me."

Rachel gaped.

"Really?"

"Yes. 'I love Michelle.' I cried."

Rachel hugged her.

"I'm so happy for both of you. Especially you, Michelle. You've sacrificed for him. I'd hate to think that he didn't understand that."

"That doesn't mean he has to love me. He could appreciate what I did for him without loving me. That's why what he said meant so much. I love him."

"He'll marry you as soon as he can."

"Are you sure?"

"Take it to the bank. Randy wants a wife. That's you."

Michelle's eyes glistened.

"That would be wonderful." She wiped her eyes. "I still haven't told Mom and Dad about the baby."

Randy joined them, wrapping his arms around Michelle. Rachel punched his arm.

"So you're in love." He grinned. "You finally found the one. You'd better treat her right or I'll beat you up." He laughed. "He issued that threat to Darren on our wedding day. He was all of fourteen."

Michelle kissed him.

"Pretty gallant for a fourteen year old."

"We were always close. Let's go in. Come on, Kenny. Lunch time."

As Randy released Michelle, a window shattered in the house.

"How'd that happen?" Michelle said.

Dirt kicked up to her left. Before her mind could process the cause, she found herself on the ground trying to catch her breath. Her body hurt. *What just happened?*

She felt herself forcibly rolled, then realized that Randy rolled with her. He had tackled her. *Why?* When they settled in a hollow in the lawn, she tried to raise her head. He pushed it down.

"What's going on?"

"Keep your heads down!" Rachel shouted. "Someone's shooting at him."

"Do you have your cell phone?"

"I'm calling now!"

Dirt jumped and sprayed Randy with dust. He placed his hand firmly on Michelle's head, then began pulling himself on his belly through the hollow.

"Randy! Get back here! Wait for the police!"

He dragged himself toward a hedge. She kept her head down while watching him. Her heart pounded. He reached the hedge and rose to a crouch. Using it for shelter, he ran toward the trees that covered the slope above the yard.

A siren sounded, at first faint, its volume increasing with each passing second. Randy disappeared into the trees.

"Where is he?" Rachel asked.

"He's after the shooter." The siren had grown loud. "Rachel, the police don't know he's up there!"

"I'm still on the phone with them. Tell your officers that my brother is up there ... Jeans and a light blue T-shirt. He can't speak ... It's okay, Michelle. She's telling them."

"He ran up there unarmed."

"He knows how to take care of himself."

Michelle prayed that Rachel was right.

A police car sped along the ridge, never slowing. They heard another patrol car in the distance. This one stopped near the end of the driveway. A third siren approached, turning into the yard. The driver cut his siren before coming across the lawn to stop beside them.

"Is anyone injured?" the officer asked when he opened the door.

They denied it.

"Is my brother okay?" Rachel asked.

"Fine. The shooter's gone. Come with me. He's trying to communicate with sign language. Maybe you can help."

He opened a back door and they climbed inside. Kenny clung to Rachel. When they reached the road, the officer pulled in beside the other police vehicle, an SUV. They found Randy helping an officer tape off the area.

"I'll stay here with Kenny," Rachel said. "You translate."

Michelle tried to open the door, then waited for the officer— Olson—to free her from the car. She hurried to Randy. Scratches covered his arms and face. His right sleeve hung tattered. He hugged her, then began waving to the south.

"He did that at first," Officer Humphrey said. "But he got frustrated and quit when I couldn't understand him. He wouldn't let me go into that area. I figured out that he wanted me to tape it off."

"Okay. Randy, what kind of vehicle was it?"

He pointed at the SUV.

"Okay. What color?"

He grabbed his T-shirt.

"Blue. That shade?"

He dropped his hand, palm down, then held his fingers an inch apart.

"A little darker?"

He touched his nose.

"Okay. A blue SUV a little darker than your shirt."

Humphrey relayed the information on the radio. Someone responded.

"I think I saw it in a driveway. Probably gone now, but I'll go back and check."

Humphrey nodded to Randy.

"Good job. Did you get a look at the suspect?"

Randy patted the back of his head.

"His back," Michelle translated.

"Tell us what you saw."

Randy walked to the SUV. After a few seconds, he placed the edge of his hand at the level of his eyebrows. Humphrey figured that out.

"A little shorter than you are. About six feet?"

Randy touched his nose. He fluffed his hair, then pointed at Olson.

"Blond. How long?"

Randy frowned, then rubbed his finger across the back of his neck.

"Shoulder length?"

The furrows in Randy's brow deepened. He tugged on the front of his hair, while drawing the line across the back.

"Just long in back?"

Randy smiled.

"Anything else?"

Randy touched his forearm.

"White. Clothes?"

He slapped his jeans, then pointed at Humphrey's shirt.

"Jeans and a tan shirt?"

Randy touched his nose.

"Long or short sleeves?"

He chopped at his wrist.

"Long sleeves. With a collar?"

Randy pointed at Humphrey's collar. Humphrey relayed the description, then grinned at Randy.

"Pretty good for a guy who can't talk."

"He can probably do better with pictures," Michelle said. "The make of the SUV, exact color, if it had New Mexico plates."

"That would help. Any idea why this guy was shooting at you?"

"Trying to finish what he started. A year ago, Randy was kidnapped. They starved and tortured him for weeks before he escaped. That's why he can't talk. Agent Lyons of the FBI is working on his case. You need to contact her. And ask her to find out where Dom Barone is."

"We'll get in touch with her. Olson will take you to the station. We have a vehicle ID program that's pretty user friendly."

Randy helped Michelle into the cruiser's back seat, then climbed in the front. Kenny leaned forward.

"Can we use the siren?"

Olson grinned.

"Doesn't look like he's any worse for wear. I can't do that, but when we get to the station, I'll let you turn it on and off real quick."

"Cool! Bet the other kids'll be sorry they had to go to school."

* * *

Darren arrived at the police station before they entered the building. He hugged his wife and son, then tried to listen to Kenny tell him about the sirens and police cars.

"Everybody's okay?" Darren asked.

"Yes. Fortunately, Kenny just thinks this is all so exciting. He was scared for a little while. But he got to ride in a police car."

"Good."

They followed Olson inside. He brought up a computer program and pointed Randy to a chair.

"Just click the right mouse button to scroll through the SUV's."

Two clicks later, Randy tapped the picture of the Jeep Cherokee.

"Good. I'll bring up the blues."

Randy selected a color called "country blue. Olson wrote on a notebook and switched to a license plate program. Without hesitation, Randy chose the Arizona plate.

"You're sure?"

Randy thumped the screen. Olson strode to the dispatcher and handed her the note.

Randy studied Michelle, his brow furrowed. He stood and guided her to the chair. She smiled.

"Yeah. I'm tired."

He rubbed her belly, the furrow deepening.

"The baby's fine."

He stood, lowered his shoulder, and slowly drove it into Darren until he took a step back.

"What's that mean?" Darren said.

"When the shooting started, he tackled me. He's worried about the baby."

"Aren't you?"

"I haven't thought about it."

"You should see a doctor," Rachel said. "Just to be safe. There's a reason pregnant women don't play football."

Michelle smiled.

"Okay. As soon as we can get away, I'll go."

Rachel accosted Olson before he returned. She gestured toward Michelle. He nodded and crossed the large room.

"Ma'am, you can use that phone to call your doctor. We'll take you to the clinic or hospital, wherever they want you."

* * *

The radiologist watched the ultrasound screen and gave instructions to the technologist. He had never attended her ultrasound before, indicating the level of concern Michelle's doctor felt.

Randy's presence also indicated his concern. He held her hand, but fidgeted, his eyes darting toward the door.

The radiologist smiled.

"Your baby's fine. You can go back to see your doctor now."

Randy managed a faint smile, then paced while she dressed. When they returned to the clinic, a nurse showed them to the doctor's office. Randy stood with his face pressed to the window. He jumped when the doctor entered.

"Is *he* alright?"

"Just a little claustrophobic."

"Well, I'll get you out of here quickly, then. Your baby is fine. You'll feel worse tomorrow. Don't worry about it. I'll see you at your next scheduled appointment."

"Thanks."

Randy bolted for the door, and barely kept his pace below a run until he reached the parking lot. He stopped by the patrol car, gasping. Michelle caught up to him and answered Officer Olson's unasked question.

"Anxiety attack. He felt a little confined. The baby and I are fine."

"Good. I'm to take you back to the Greene's. I believe Mr. Mc Kay's parents have arranged for someone to escort you to their ranch from there."

XXVIII.

They stayed overnight with Rachel and Darren while patrol cars cruised the neighborhood. In the morning, two off-duty Mora County deputies followed them back to the ranch.

Michelle eased herself from the Explorer while Randy hurried around to help her. Kendall and Liz seemed to appear out of nowhere.

"How are you?" Kendall asked.

"Oh, I feel like I've been playing football without pads. I see you're packing heat."

"I've armed everyone on the place who knows how to use a hand gun."

Randy slapped his hip, then pointed at the pistol.

"You want a gun?"

Randy touched his nose.

"You know how to handle one. I don't see why not. I'll get you one later this morning. Michelle, you should probably lay down."

"I think I'll soak in the tub first."

Randy hovered all the way to the bathroom, then filled the tub for her. He helped her undress. She kissed him softly.

"I know you feel bad, but you were protecting me. Better to get tackled than shot."

A corner of his mouth turned up. He lifted her into the tub, then sat on the edge.

"Want to join me?"

He grinned, but it faded.

"I know. I'm too stiff to be much fun. Do you realize that you're answering 'yes' when people ask you a question?"

His brow furrowed.

"Don't doubt me. You touch your nose. That's a 'yes' if I ever saw one. I'll ask you an easy 'yes' question. Do you like sex?"

Randy grinned and touched his nose.

"There. I don't know why you can't nod your head, but if this works, great. Now we need something that works for 'no.' Touch your chin."

He shrugged and obeyed.

"Okay. Now an easy question. Do you like Susan?"

Randy touched his chin.

"Promising. Let's work on this some more. Do you like riding?"

He touched his nose.

"Is your name Randy?"

Nose.

"Are you 39?"

Chin.

"Do you love me?"

Yes.

"Are we living in Wyoming?"

No.

"Are we living in Arizona?"

No.

"Are we living in New Mexico?"

Yes.

"Am I going to cry now?"

Yes.

Randy kissed her, then wiped her tears.

"Oh, Randy. This is so huge. This is so great for you."

After another kiss, he began washing her. Michelle's tears subsided.

"I love you, Randy. I think you'll be yourself in no time."

* * *

Michelle climbed out of bed when she heard Kendall in the kitchen.

"You didn't have to get up for me. Randy and I can get along without you."

Michelle smiled.

"I wanted to show you how right you are. Ask Randy some 'yes' and 'no' questions."

"O-kay. Ah-h. Is this the gun you wanted?"

Randy touched his nose. Michelle translated.

"Did you recognize the guy who shot at you?"

No.

"He came from Arizona. Do you have any idea who he might be?"

No.

"Will you stick close to the ranch for a while?"

Yes.

Kendall bit his lip.

"It's nice to be able to carry on a conversation with you, son. Your mom's going to bawl her head off."

Randy rolled his eyes. Michelle squeezed him.

"I cried too."

"I talked to Agent Lyons this morning. She found out that Barone was seen in Arizona yesterday. He couldn't be the shooter."

"When I stopped to think about it, he would have had to wear a disguise. Randy said the shooter was blond."

"Randy, she'd probably like to talk to you now that you can answer some questions."

Randy shifted from one foot to the other. No.

"Not ready for that yet. But soon. They need your help catching these guys."

Yes.

"Good. I'll give your mom the good news. I'll keep her away until she gets her emotions under control."

"Tell her I'm resting," Michelle said.

* * *

"Randy's thirtieth birthday is April 10th," Liz said to Michelle over lunch a few days later.

"Thirty is a big deal. Are you planning a party?"

"Yes. Would you like to help me?"

"Of course. Will this be a surprise party?"

"Do you think that would be a good idea?"

"Probably not. He still doesn't care for surprises."

"How about if we tell him the day before?"

"That would work."

"I've already invited his four closest friends from Arizona. I knew they'd need extra time to arrange their schedule. I explained Randy's condition and told them if they weren't comfortable, they should stay away. All four plan to attend."

"Did you contact them after he started communicating?"

"No. That will be a nice surprise for them. Along with your pregnancy."

"He's living a man's dream come true. No job to go to. A woman catering to his every whim. They'll be jealous."

"Should I invite your parents to this party?"

"No!" Michelle sipped water. "I mean, I haven't told them about the baby yet."

"Oh. Are you ashamed of your pregnancy?"

Michelle pushed her plate aside.

"I feel guilty."

"You did a wonderful thing for Randy. Try not to lose sight of that."

"I'll try."

"I'd hoped he'd be able to speak at the party. But there's still plenty of reason to celebrate this year."

"That's right. He would have been missing on his birthday last year."

"Yes. That was an awful day. All the more reason to celebrate."

"Since he's spending more time with Kendall, I *can* actually help plan. He's not with me every minute."

"How do you feel about that?"

"Good. I've had time to get used to it. We both need him to be independent."

"It's easy to want to shelter him. But Randy has been his own man for a very long time. They took that from him. You gave it back."

"I just supported him."

"You've worked miracles. I'd like to give you something."

Michelle opened her mouth to argue, but Liz rose, gesturing for her to come. Michelle followed her out of the dining room and upstairs to the huge master bedroom. Liz led her to a five-foot-tall jewelry armoire, and pulled out a tray of rings, placing it on a small table.

"That's where you get all the rings."

"Oh, I don't even wear these anymore. My favorites are on another tray. I'd like you to have one or more. Since I wear them on every finger, you should be able to find something that fits you."

"I've never worn much jewelry. I never had a reason to." Michelle slipped several rings on and off her left ring finger. "Oh, I hope this one fits."

"It's you. I hope so too."

The silver and turquoise horse slid on her finger. She smiled. "I love it."

"It's perfect for you. Take more, if you like."

"No, thanks. One is more my style."

XXIX.

Michelle caressed Randy's cheek.

"Are you nervous?"

Yes.

"Everyone knows what to expect from you. Your mom told them to stay away if they couldn't handle it."

He gave a quick grin.

"What did that mean?"

He shrugged, still smiling.

"I've gotten pretty good at reading you. What do you know that I don't?"

He kept smiling.

"We'd better go. Everyone should be there."

His smile faded and he took a deep breath. He wrapped his arm around her on the way to his parents' house. Two dozen people applauded when they entered the livingroom. Randy smiled, but dropped his head. His hold on her tightened.

Another deep breath and he released her, meeting the eyes of his party guests. He began circulating, shaking hands with everyone and hugging most. Michelle shadowed him, introducing herself when he gestured to her.

Carlos grinned, pointed at Michelle's belly, and addressed Randy.

"Did you do that?"

Randy returned the grin. Yes.

"Well, now. Big improvement over the last time I saw you. Guess everything works except the voice. Suppose you'll be coming back to work before we know it."

Randy turned serious. No. Carlos pondered that.

"Do you mean it will be a long time before you come back to work?"

No.

"You mean you're not coming back at all?"

Yes.

"Is this what we talked about? You're going into the newspaper business?"

Yes.

"Can't say I blame you."

Michelle tried to control her voice.

"What's this about, Carlos?"

"He needed to prove himself before he went into the family business. A couple years ago, he decided that he'd done that. Figured he'd learn the newspaper business sometime after he turned thirty."

"Thank God." Both Randy and Carlos gave her puzzled looks. "Okay. I'm relieved. I like the idea of you having a job where people don't see you as a threat."

Randy hugged her and kissed her neck. Carlos chuckled.

"Can't blame you for that either. You got your baby to think of."

* * *

Later, Michelle noticed Randy arguing with his father. Randy extended his hand, palm up. Kendall shook his head. She thought he said, "Not now." Randy extended his hand a little farther. Kendal refused. Randy poked his finger into his palm. Kendall sighed and handed him a small object.

She smiled. Randy could wear a person down.

He turned toward her, and swallowed. He took a step, then stopped. Finally, he crossed the room.

"Why are you so nervous?"

The corners of his mouth turned up briefly. He bit his lip, then let his breath out and dropped to one knee. Michelle stepped back. He opened the small box and held it out. She covered her mouth with both hands, staring at the ample diamond. It sparkled even more through her tears. She nodded.

"Yes. I'll marry you."

He grinned, rose, and hugged her, while the guests applauded again. He removed the turquoise ring and slipped the diamond on her finger. She wiped her tears.

"Your mom knew about this."

Yes. He kissed her.

Liz joined them.

"I'm so happy for both of you. When Randy wanted to get you a ring, we asked him how he'd know what size to get. It took him a while to explain his plan."

"Quite a plan. I didn't suspect a thing."

Kendall walked up behind Liz.

"He found a picture of a wedding ring and about wore it out. I thought he should wait until he could talk. But he insisted. When I finally consented to take him shopping, he even had a plan for figuring out your ring size. I guess he's serious."

"Of course, he's serious," Liz said. "He finally found a woman who loves him, not his money."

"I disagreed with his timing. What if Michelle had refused?"

"You must be joking."

"Refused?" Michelle said. "Why would I refuse?"

"I like to cover all my bases. And I suppose I'm a little over-protective."

"I love Randy. I loved him before I decided to have his baby. I've been waiting—hoping—for this. It's a dream come true."

＊ ＊ ＊

Michelle took a deep breath, staring at the phone. Randy, seated by her side, handed it to her. She sighed.

"Yes. I suppose. I need to get it over with." She punched the number. "Hi, Mom."

"Hello, stranger. They must be keeping you busy down there. These calls are getting few and far between."

"Sorry. I've had a lot of things on my mind."

"Is something wrong?"

"No. Are you sitting down?"

"What's wrong?"

"Sit down."

She heard a chair slide across the floor.

"Okay."

"Mom, Randy asked me to marry him."

"Marry. Can he talk?"

"No. But he got down on one knee and gave me a huge diamond."

"That's a proposal in any language. But, Michelle, he can't marry you if he can't communicate. He could get so frustrated before then." Michelle did not reply. "He has no reason to be frustrated."

"No."

"Oh, Michelle. Did he force himself on you?"

"No. Technically, I forced myself on him."

A long pause.

"Why, Michelle?"

"Because I love him. And I thought it might help."

"How do his parents feel about this?"

"They want him to be happy. Liz is really enthused. Kendall's more lukewarm. Mom, I'm pregnant." The silence lasted so long that she continued. "I know you're disappointed in me. I'm sorry."

"Oh, Michelle. I'm disappointed that you didn't give the Lord time to work miracles. But I was just thinking about how far you've come. I was so afraid you'd end up old and alone. It's hard to imagine that you're going to have a baby. Are you sure Randy loves you?"

Michelle squeezed his hand.

"Very. He's said it." She explained about the sentences. "And I see it in his eyes."

"I'm happy for you."

"How will Dad take this?"

"Don't worry about that. You won't have to deal with it. We can work it out here."

"He'll be mad."

"Don't worry about it. Understand? Let me take care of it."

"I'll try not to."

"When are you due?"

"September 10th."

"I'll come after you get home from the hospital."

XXX.

"Everything is fine, Miss Bowman," the doctor said. "We'll see you again in two weeks."

Michelle thanked him and Randy wrapped his arm around her on the way to the lobby.

"I need to stop at the pharmacy for pre-natal vitamins."

He held up the car keys and shook them.

"Good idea. I'd appreciate getting into an air conditioned vehicle today."

When she stepped outside a few minutes later, the heat made everything harder, as if she carried a hundred pound weight. Sweat almost instantly formed on her forehead. She looked around for the Explorer. Randy had dropped her at the door before he parked.

A car window shattered next to her. Michelle dropped to the ground. If she learned later that the window had shattered spontaneously from the heat, fine. Until then, she would assume that bullets shattered windows.

She heard two pops, another window shattered, then a thud, proving her theory.

Tires squealed. Randy hesitated beside her long enough to see that she had not been hit, then the tires squealed again. She heard another vehicle speed away. Unsilenced gunfire. Randy's gun.

More squealing tires, then a transmission whining in reverse. Randy braked to a halt and rocketed from the vehicle.

"I'm fine."

He caressed her here and there, his hands never stopping.

"I'm fine. Really. I think I just got some glass down my neck."

"The police are on their way!" a woman said. "Are you okay?" Michelle repeated her report. "Come inside. We'll check you for cuts. And it's a cooler place to wait for the police."

They could already hear a siren. Randy waved Michelle inside, then pointed at the ground.

"You're staying out here?"

Yes.

"Okay. I won't be long if you need me to interpret."

A patrol car screeched into the parking lot right after Michelle entered the building. Officer Humphrey leaped out.

"Mr. Mc Kay, Darren told me how you can answer questions. Was it the same guy?"

Yes.

"Same vehicle?"

No. Randy hurried from one vehicle to another, starting with the car with the broken window. Humphrey interpreted with very few mistakes. Within three minutes, he broadcast Randy's description.

"All units. Be on the lookout for a bronze late model Dodge four by four pickup with a shattered back window. New Mexico plates. Consider the driver armed and dangerous. He's suspected in the shots fired at the clinic today and an earlier shooting."

Michelle returned. She looked from Randy to Humphrey.

"Did you need help?"

"No. He gave a good description of the vehicle. Somebody *really* dislikes him. Good thing they're a lousy shot."

Her jaw dropped and her eyes met Randy's. His scowl softened. He pulled her close.

"They were shooting at *me*. Randy was nowhere near me. Why would anyone want to shoot me?"

Randy kissed her forehead while Humphrey pondered that.

"Could you have been the target last time?"

"I-I suppose. I was right next to Randy. Why would anyone want to shoot me?"

"Maybe because you're important to Mr. Mc Kay. Maybe they think he'll fall apart with you out of the picture."

"I suppose. It's not true. But someone could believe that."

"Let's go over what happened."

Randy pointed at the clinic, then the sky. Michelle agreed.

"I'm kind of wilting out here."

"We don't want to disturb their business any more than we have to. When another unit gets here, we'll go down to the station. You want to sit in your vehicle till then?"

"Yes."

The cruiser's radio interrupted them. An officer reported that he was in pursuit of the suspect vehicle. They crowded around the open door.

The suspect left the Taos city limits. Dead air. The pickup turned off the paved road. Then nothing. The dispatcher called for another report. Three times. Finally, the officer broke his silence. He reported his car hung up in ruts and the suspect headed south through rugged country.

Randy slammed his fist on the roof of the car. Humphrey swore.

Another patrol car arrived about the same time as the owner of the bullet-riddled car came from the clinic. Humphrey gave instructions to the other officer, then told Randy and Michelle to follow him to the police station.

✳ ✳ ✳

When they arrived, Randy immediately gestured to Michelle, indicating that she needed to relax and put her feet up. Humphrey nodded.

"Is he right, ma'am?"

"Well, I suppose. My back aches and my ankles are swollen."

"There's a couch in this office. You'll be more comfortable."

"Thanks."

Randy held her hand while she recounted what she remembered.

"Thank you, ma'am. Tell me about your enemies."

"I don't have any enemies."

"Everyone has enemies. People who really don't like them."

"Well, there's the guy who sexually assaulted me. But he's back in prison in Wyoming. He made the mistake of trying to hurt me last summer. Randy beat him to a pulp."

"Was he seriously injured?"

"Broken nose. Broken jaw. He spent some time in a hospital before he went back to prison."

"What about his friends or relatives?"

"During and after his trial they were pretty vocal. His father especially. He figured that by going on a date with him, I was agreeing to sex. He thought his son had the right to expect it of me. And, anyhow, since I managed to fight him off, he hadn't raped me, so no harm done. He thought I was being vindictive."

"That sounds like an enemy to me."

"I suppose. But we didn't hear a peep out of him after his son ended up in the hospital."

"Still, we'll have the Wyoming authorities check into his whereabouts. They can decide if they need to investigate any other relatives. Any other enemies?"

"No-o." Michelle grinned. "I guess Randy's sister really doesn't like me."

Randy laughed. Humphrey gave her a quizzical look.

"Rachel?"

"No. His other sister. Susan."

"Oh. That's it?"

"I don't get around much. Doesn't give me many chances to make enemies."

"Well, it's just a question we have to ask. I'd bet this has nothing to do with your enemies. It's all about Mr. Mc Kay. You rest here. I'll see if I can get in touch with the FBI."

Michelle leaned her head back and closed her eyes. She was not sure how much time passed before Humphrey returned.

"I just spoke to Agent Lyons. She wants you to stay here until she comes."

"Here? At the station? How long will that be?"

"She's in the area on another case. About an hour."

"Oh. I guess I can rest here that long. Any longer and I should probably go to Rachel's and lay down."

Randy tapped his nose several times.

"Maybe that's not such a bad idea, ma'am," Humphrey said. "You look beat. I'll call Agent Lyons and tell her to meet you there."

Yes.

Michelle smiled.

"You talked me into it."

* * *

"Why wasn't I informed that Mr. Mc Kay could answer questions?"

Randy patted his chest. Michelle sought a more comfortable position in the recliner.

"Like he said, it was his decision. He wasn't ready to talk to you."

Agent Lyons scowled at Randy.

"This might not have happened if you'd talked to me."

Randy's brow furrowed and he shrugged.

"Very well. You saw two of your kidnapers. Were there more than two?"

Yes.

"Were there more than three?"

No.

"Did you see the third kidnaper?"

No.

"Was the third kidnaper ever at the cabin where you were held?"

Yes.

"Did they blindfold you when this person came?"

Yes.

"So we can assume that he was someone you knew. Did you hear him speak?"

No.

"Did he take part in the torture?"

Randy shuddered. Yes. Yes. He clenched his fists. Lyons gave him a moment.

"Was he there often?"

No.

"More than once?"

No.

"Did you kill the other two kidnapers?"

Randy's eyes widened. No.

"They were killed with your gun. Apparently their accomplice tied up loose ends and tried to make it look like you did the deed. I have a lot of other questions, but they would all require answers that you can't give."

Michelle interrupted.

"He's very good at charades. You might give that a try."

Lyons chewed her lip.

"Can you explain how you escaped?"

Yes. Randy left the room and returned with Rachel. He stood her beside Lyons.

"What's this about?" Rachel asked.

"Your brother is explaining how he escaped."

He guided Rachel back to the door and waved to her.

"Are you saying that one of the kidnapers left?"

Yes. He rolled up a newspaper and pretended to hit Lyons over the head with it.

"You hit the other one."

Yes.

"That gives us a time frame. The medical examiner estimated that the bruise to his head occurred no more than 48 hours pre-mortem. How did you get free to hit him? They must have had you tied."

Yes. Randy's brow furrowed. He held his palms parallel, decreased the space between them, and at the same time sucked in his cheeks.

"You lost so much weight that you were able to get loose?"

Randy smiled. Yes.

"You *are* pretty good at this."

"We communicate," Michelle said. "What I'd really like to know is how he traveled the hundred miles to our ranch."

Randy grinned and left the room. He returned a few minutes later with the engine from Kenny's toy train.

"You hopped a freight train?"

Yes.

"That solves that mystery."

Lyons drummed her fingers on the arm of her chair.

"Do you have any idea who the other man was?"

No.

"Have you given it any thought?"

Yes.

"Did this sniper seem at all familiar to you?"

No.

"He could be the other kidnaper, or he could be hired muscle just like the other two. Whoever's behind this doesn't just want you dead. He has a pathological hatred for you. He wanted to inflict as much suffering as possible. I believe this attack on Miss Bowman is another example of that hatred. She's a target because she's important to you. She may have been the target the first time he shot at you."

Randy and Michelle looked at each other. Finally, Michelle spoke.

"I thought of that today."

"That should narrow down the list of suspects. Mr. Mc Kay, who hates you that much?"

He ran his hand through his hair, then shrugged.

"The case you were working on before you were kidnapped. Did you uncover anything that you didn't have time to put into a report?"

No.

Lyons sighed.

"That case was a long shot anyhow. The people involved would have just killed you. It would have been business. Are you taking extra security precautions?"

Yes. Michelle explained.

"Randy's father and his foreman are on their way. They'll give us an armed escort back to the ranch. We feel safe there."

"And that's a good point. Both attacks have been here. I need a list of the people who know when you come here."

"We try not to tell anyone except Randy's parents and Rachel. But everybody who works at the ranch sees us leave. They all know where we're going, because this is the *only* place we go. Do you think someone at the ranch is involved?"

"I'd bet on it. I've been to that ranch. No one could be watching from a neighbor's place. There isn't one."

Randy scowled. Michelle shuddered.

"Do you think we're in danger from that person?"

"It's possible. Mr. Mc Kay, do any of your father's employees have a beef with you?"

Randy thought about it. No.

"Maybe one of them has a criminal record you don't know about. I'll run a background check when you get me that list. Include all the employees, even if you think they wouldn't know when you leave."

XXXI.

Even with the knowledge that there could be a spy at the ranch, Michelle felt safe there. Kendall faxed the list to Agent Lyons, but personally vouched for all the men he had armed. And he supported Randy's belief.

"The men carrying guns have all been with us at least fourteen years, so they knew Randy as a teenager. He didn't expect any special treatment from them and he never debauched any of their daughters, sisters, or girlfriends. They shouldn't have a grudge against him."

Randy grinned. Michelle smiled.

"But you can't say the same for the men you didn't arm?"

"I wouldn't swear to it. He was rich and good-looking. Most girls thought that made up for his being a jerk. My teenaged years look pretty tame by comparison."

Randy chuckled. She shook her finger at him.

"That better be behind you."

He made a cross over his heart, smiling. Then he hugged her.

"Oh, you can barely get your arms around me anymore."

Kendall chuckled.

"How is that grandchild of mine?"

"Rowdy. I already have to nap when he does. He keeps me awake day and night. I think we're both in for some sleepless nights after he's born."

"It won't be long now."

"Three weeks. Maybe he'll come early. I hope he comes early."

"After he comes, we can hire a nanny. There's no need for you to lose sleep."

"A nanny?"

"Of course."

"No."

Kendall studied her, while Randy kissed her forehead and squeezed her a little tighter. Kendall shrugged.

"Well, remember you have that option. I'd better get to work. Randy, are you still sticking close to Michelle?"

Yes.

"I'll see you later. Come to dinner this evening."

"Thanks. We will." Michelle waited until he left. "*A nanny!* I can raise my own child. Were you raised by a nanny?"

Yes. No.

"You had a nanny?"

Yes.

"That's probably why you were such a tomcat in high school."

He grinned. Yes.

"You're teasing me. A woman who doesn't leave the house to go to a job shouldn't need a nanny. And if that sounds like I'm criticizing your mom, I am."

He laughed and kissed her.

＊ ＊ ＊

"We've found the sniper," Agent Lyons said.

Michelle gripped the phone.

"Is he dead?"

"How did you know?"

"He failed twice. I'm surprised his employer gave him the second chance."

"True. There's no doubt about his identity. We found both vehicles as well."

"Randy's kidnaper has killed three people already, he's probably really ticked off about all these failures, and he still hates Randy. This isn't over."

"Not by any stretch of the imagination. Does Mr. Mc Kay remember any other details?"

She looked at Randy, hanging on her end of the conversation. "Agent Lyons wants to know if you remember anything else."

No.

"He says nothing new."

"Contact me if that changes. Stay alert. I'll check back with you in a week, unless I get a break in the case between now and then."

"Thanks." Michelle disconnected. "She wants to hear from us if you remember anything at all." He took her hand. "Where are we going?"

He smiled and led her toward the bathroom, where he began filling the tub. He unbuttoned her blouse.

"A soak in the tub sounds great. But I'm not sure I can get down there. And once I get down, I know I can't get up again."

He placed a palm on his chest.

"You're going to help me. Okay. Just don't hurt yourself."

He laughed.

* * *

Michelle walked around the kitchen, rubbing her lower back for the third time since breakfast. Randy looked up from his lunch and pointed to her plate.

"I know I should eat, but I just can't get comfortable. I usually have a backache, but nothing like this one."

He rose, his brow furrowed, and placed his hand on her belly.

"The baby's fine. He's busy as ever."

No. He arched his hand downward, then held his arms as if he cradled a baby. Michelle took a moment to catch on.

"You think I'm in labor?"

Yes.

"I still have two weeks until my due date."

He raised his palms, shoulders, and eyebrows.

"Okay. So that doesn't mean anything. I've never been in labor. I suppose I could be."

He pointed at the door.

"Your parents said we shouldn't go without them. Is your dad home today?"

Yes.

"Go get them. I'll get my overnight bag. No hurry. If I'm in labor, it's early."

Michelle retrieved her bag from the bedroom. When she returned to the kitchen, Randy and his parents rushed in.

"Randy says the baby's coming now," Kendall said.

"No. He was trying to tell you I might be in labor. We should go have the doctor check."

Kendall let his breath out.

"Oh. I had visions of delivering a baby half way to Taos."

"Well, if we stand around here talking," Liz said. "We still might. We don't need to speed, but let's not dawdle."

Kendall chuckled.

"Why take chances? I'll drive."

✴ ✴ ✴

The doctor pronounced Michelle in early labor. She and Randy walked the halls of the hospital while hours passed. At first, she worried about his claustrophobia. But it seemed not to bother him at all.

By evening, concern for him no longer crossed her mind.

"Will this ever end?" she snapped.

He did not reply, having had her irritation turned on him more than once. She dropped to a chair, her face contorted with her first major contraction. He darted to her side and held her hand while she breathed through it. He brushed the damp hair off her forehead.

"Thanks. Maybe it won't be long now. I love you."

He placed his hand over his heart.

After that, her labor progressed rapidly. At 8:32, Michelle gave birth to an eight pound, two ounce boy. Randy, tears in his eyes, caressed his son. He kissed her. She said nothing, just marveling at the miracle in her arms.

An hour later, Randy held the baby when Kendall and Liz came to see their new grandson. Liz cried too.

"Oh, he's beautiful. What's his name?"

"Robert Randall Mc Kay."

"Randy, did you help pick the name?"

Yes.

"I kept bouncing names off him until he agreed," Michelle said. "He didn't want a Randy, junior."

"Liz wanted to name Randy, Kendall, junior," Kendall said. "I agree with him. Children should have their own name. And it's just a lot easier in the long run."

Michelle yawned.

"It's been a long day. If I have one more day like today, we'll only have two kids."

Randy kissed her forehead, then waved his parents away.

"Randy's right," Kendall said. "We need to let you rest. You'll feel more like company tomorrow. We'll go and let Rachel have a quick look at him. Have you called your parents?"

"Yeah. They won't be able to come for at least a week. They may bring some of my nieces and nephews. They've missed me."

"The more, the merrier. We have room for your whole family."

XXXII.

Robert proved Michelle right, taking short naps day and night, waking them frequently. Randy helped as much as he could, changing the baby and bringing him to her to nurse. Still, she felt exhausted. Sometimes she could not stay awake until Robert finished eating. Randy took him back to his crib.

When she dozed, she dreamed about Randy. He said, "I love you." and she smiled in her sleep.

A week after Robert's birth, she woke with the sun already up and Randy gone. He had let her sleep in. She smiled and took her time preparing for the day, knowing that her son would soon demand her attention. She made it to the kitchen without hearing from him.

Robert slept in his seat while Randy read the newspaper. He rose, kissed her, and poured coffee.

"Thanks." She sipped her coffee and settled into her chair. "And thanks for letting me sleep in."

"I love you."

Michelle stared.

"Am I hallucinating?"

"No. I love you."

"You can talk?"

"Yes. Almost as good as I used to."

Tears ran down her cheeks.

"How?"

"I don't know. Something just clicked when Robby was born. I knew I could talk. I didn't want to say anything until I had a chance to practice. I wanted 'I love you' to be the first thing you heard from me."

"I love you, Randy."

She stood and threw her arms around his neck, sobbing. He gave her a moment to collect herself.

"Once in awhile, there's a glitch. I just stop. If I try to force it, I stutter. I just have to wait it out. And, how's this for bizarre? I still can't nod. I mean, I can, physically. But not in response to a question. I asked myself all kinds of yes and no questions. Couldn't do it."

"Wow. I'd like somebody to try to explain *that*."

"No kidding. Now that I can talk, there are a few things I need to do. The most important is to marry you. But I need to talk ... to Agent Lyons too."

Michelle's sobbing resumed.

"How soon can we get married?"

"That's entirely up to you. Have the kind of wedding you want. If you want an elaborate wedding, it'll take longer. I'll only offer this. I know what you gave up for me. I won't make love to you again until after we're married. I can make that sacrifice for you."

"So you'd like a quick wedding."

"It doesn't matter. I can wait as long as it takes. You've given enough. I'll have the rest of my life to make love to you."

"I've thought about our wedding."

"I saw you looking at the magazines."

"I have some ideas."

"Mom can get a wedding planner. She probably already has one in mind."

"Probably. I have so many questions for you."

"Ask."

"When you came to us, how did you see the world?"

"Good question. Emotionally. I was afraid of almost everything. Even you. But you gained my trust and I latched on to you. I only felt safe with you. I know you thought I was childlike. But I never felt like a child."

"And you couldn't understand anything that we said?"

"No. When I first heard you talk, I thought, somehow, I'd ended up in a foreign country. But when I wanted to ask if anyone spoke English, nothing happened. I knew something was terribly wrong. I noticed the Wyoming plates on your vehicles. Couldn't figure out how I got to Wyoming."

"But you did later."

"Yeah. Learning to understand you was like learning a new language cold. You're a good teacher, by the way."

"I'm sorry."

"Sorry? For what?"

"For seducing you."

He laughed.

"Do you know how much I wanted to be seduced? You know how it feels when something's slipped your mind? I felt that way about my life. You kept bringing things back to me. I knew there was something I could do that would feel really good. I just couldn't remember what it was. I even looked for a picture in your magazines. But you had the wrong kind of magazines."

"I thought I'd scarred you for life."

"You helped me feel like a man again. I'm sorry that I couldn't remember the right way to do it. I know you were in pain. I'm really sorry about that."

"You didn't know better. I made my choice. It wasn't your fault."

"It wasn't your fault either. You were a virgin. You didn't know what to expect. You didn't deserve that."

"It doesn't matter now. I'll be your wife. That's all that matters."

He kissed her forehead.

"My first virgin is my wife. Isn't that ironic?"

"Your first? Not even when you were a teenager?"

"I was too selfish to take the time to talk a girl out of her virginity. Give me an experienced girl who knew how to please me. That was my philosophy."

"I see. You need to tell your parents that you can talk."

"That's my first stop. I'll go as soon as you're okay."

"I'm fine. Robby will want to be fed before long. Go talk to your parents. Just hurry home."

He smiled and kissed her.

"This isn't home. Now we can start planning ours. We'll build it on that hill where I always stop when we ride."

"What a great view. How long have you been thinking about this?"

"I've known I wanted my house there for ten years. It's my favorite spot. I'll be back shortly."

"Make sure your mom is sitting down."

He laughed.

* * *

When Randy reached his parents kitchen, he listened to Kendall while he waited for Liz to sit. But she flitted around the kitchen for so long that he guided her to a chair.

"Mom, you need to sit down for this."

She fainted. Kendall sputtered while Randy patted her face, trying to rouse her. Finally, Kendall found his voice.

"When?"

"After Robby was born. I've been practicing until today."

Liz stirred.

"Randy?"

"Yeah, Mom, I can talk again." She burst into tears. "That's about how Michelle responded. But she didn't faint."

"Oh, this is wonderful. You're back."

"I was always here. Even when I didn't recognize you, I knew who I was."

"You need to talk to the FBI," Kendall said.

"I know. I'll call when ... I leave here. That happens every once in a while. I just have to wait it out. Michelle and I are getting married as soon as she can plan a wedding."

"Are you sure, son? Now that you can talk, you might meet someone else."

Randy covered his face and shook his head.

"I spent years trying to meet someone. All I found were gold diggers. God dropped me in Michelle's lap without even a shirt on my back. She loves *me*, not my money. I couldn't have picked anyone better. Not even close."

"Randy's right," Liz said. "Michelle's a blessing. She's a better daughter-in-law than I deserve. I never thought any woman would be good enough for Randy, but she is."

"I'm not good enough for her. But I'll sure try to be. Dad, can I borrow some of those architecture magazines? We need to plan a house."

XXXIII.

"Imagine my surprise," Agent Lyons said, sitting in Michelle and Randy's kitchen. "When I was told that Randy Mc Kay wanted to speak to me."

Randy smiled.

"It was a shock to everyone."

"Let's start from the beginning." She placed a recorder on the table. "Tell me about your abduction."

"I was just coming back from my ride. It was a weekday, so I hadn't seen anyone. About a quarter-mile from the campground, I met a man walking. When I got close to him, he pulled a gun. He pointed out his buddy with a rifle on the slope above me. He told me to dismount. If I tried anything, they'd shoot Goldie."

"They threatened the horse, not you?"

"Yeah."

"Who knows that the horse is important to you?"

"Anybody who knows me. I have—had a picture of him on my desk. I talk about horses a lot. If they know me, they know about my horse."

"I see. So someone who knows you well is involved."

Randy looked at Michelle and let his breath out.

"I've been avoiding that thought. Did your background check turn up anything?"

"Nothing worse than traffic tickets. I even checked into the citizenship of your Hispanic employees. An illegal might succumb to pressure. But they're all citizens. Go on."

"I dismounted and he took my gun. He cuffed my hands behind my back. They walked me back to the campground to an old Blazer with Utah plates. Goldie followed. They put duct tape over my mouth, shoved me in the back, then taped my ankles together. They threw a blanket over me and stuff on top of that. I was ..."

"Go on."

Randy explained about his pauses.

"I was under that blanket for hours. When they pulled me out, it was dark, but the moon was out. I could see that I was at a cabin in the woods. There was snow on the ground. They recuffed my hands in front of me and tied me to a rafter. After they ate, they started torturing me. Took my shirt and shoes and whipped me, then went to bed. In the morning, they had breakfast, then burned me with cigarettes. That was their ... pattern. Eat, then torture me. The third night, they tied me in a chair. They thought I might be quieter there. My groaning kept them awake."

"And they never asked you anything?"

"They treated me like a thing. They ignored anything I said. The second day, they gave me water because they said I wouldn't last without it. The third morning they gave me some bread. I got something to eat and drink once a day. Bread, chips, crackers. Usually stale."

"When did the third man show up?"

"It was at least two weeks. Probably ... closer to three." Randy rubbed his hands over his face. "That was the worst day. All three took turns. All day."

"Are you sure that the other man participated?"

"Yeah. Because one of the guys said, 'You really enjoy this, don't you.' The other person must have wanted to use the jumper cables on me. They said, 'You wouldn't like that as much. It knocks him out.' They didn't use them that day. They maybe only did that to me a half-dozen times. I didn't suffer enough when I passed out."

"And they never said anything to indicate why you were being tortured?"

"No. It got so bad that I begged them to ask me something. They just smirked. Didn't even bother to laugh. After that, I started shutting down. I knew that it hurt, because my muscles still tried to ... pull away. But the pain didn't register. I remember them noticing that. One of them even talked about killing me, because the torture wasn't affecting me anymore. The other one said they were getting paid by the day. The longer I lived, the more they made. It's about the last thing I ... understood."

"Let's go back to the other man. The one you didn't see. Anything you remember? Sounds? Smells? Anything at all?"

Randy's brow furrowed.

"A smoker. That person especially liked cigarette burns. Blew smoke on me between burns."

"Go on."

He closed his eyes for a moment. They flew open, darting around the room. He focused on Michelle, who came to his rescue.

"I think he needs a break."

"He remembers something."

"He'll still remember after a break. Maybe better."

Lyons sighed and turned off her recorder.

"I'll be outside."

After she left, Michelle hugged him and stroked his hair.

"You're shaking. What do you remember?"

He let his breath out.

"Perfume."

"Perfume? The other kidnapper was a woman?"

"It was *Susan*."

She stepped back. She wanted to ask him if he was sure, but his eyes answered that question.

"She hates you that much?"

"Yes."

"You need to tell Agent Lyons."

"She'll think I'm a paranoid lunatic. That means Susan's also a murderer. Who's going to believe that?"

"I believe it. Tell her."

Michelle opened the door and Lyons returned. She flipped on the recorder.

"What do you remember?"

"The other person was my sister, Susan."

Lyons drummed her fingers on the table.

"She's a viable suspect."

"You've considered her?" Michelle said.

"I read your statement to the Taos police. You mentioned her when asked about your enemies."

"I was joking."

"Sometimes an offhand comment points us in the right direction. Mr. Mc Kay, why do you suspect your sister?"

"I don't suspect her. I know it was her."

"Why?"

"Because she's tried to kill me twice before."

Michelle gripped his shoulder and Lyons stared. The silence dragged on for more than a minute. Lyons spoke slowly.

"Explain, please."

"When I was five, she pushed me into a flooding creek. If Dad hadn't been downstream, I'd have drowned. She told him I fell in. She even convinced me it was an accident. Said she bumped into me."

"How old was she at the time?"

"Must have been eighteen."

"You said she convinced you that it was an accident. When did you change your mind?"

"The second time. When I was eleven. We were riding along a trail with a steep drop off. She shoved me off my horse. I would have gone over the edge if I hadn't grabbed his mane. She ... said that if I told anyone, they wouldn't believe me. They'd never believe anything I said again. I didn't tell anyone, but I didn't trust her anymore. When she was home, I locked my door. I wouldn't ... be alone with her. I went to extremes to avoid it."

"And even into adulthood, you never told anyone?"

"No. Once I got bigger and stronger than she was, I felt safe. When we argued and no one was around, I'd remind her that I wasn't a little kid anymore. I underestimated just how much she hates me."

Lyons drummed the table again.

"We've discretely investigated her. 'Win at all costs' best describes her. I'm surprised that she hasn't had any brushes with the law. These previous attempts fit into that pathological hatred for you. What other motive can explain trying to murder a child?"

"What will you do?"

"Dig deeper. But quietly. We'll search for a connection between her and the three dead men. Now that we know where to look, we should be able to find something."

"What should we do?"

"Go about your lives. We still believe that she has a spy here. So don't share this information with anyone."

"Not even my parents?"

"No. They'll find this hard to believe. Wait until we have more than your word."

"Do you believe me?"

"Yes, I do, Captain Mc Kay. You wouldn't accuse your own sister if you had any doubts."

Randy sighed.

"I think I knew all along. I just couldn't admit it to myself."

XXXIV.

Randy made himself scarce around the time Michelle's parents were expected. They, along with all her nieces and nephews, spent an hour fussing over Robby before Randy entered the kitchen, sweat stained and dusty.

The kids ran to him. He offered hugs and smiles, but did not look at Les and Bev. While the kids asked him questions, Bev handed Robby back to Michelle. She pushed through her grandchildren to give Randy a hug. He squeezed her.

"I'm sorry."

"No, Randy. You did the best you could at the time. You're doing the right thing now. That ring means a lot to us."

"I love her. You all saved my life."

"We love you too, Randy. You're already a member of our family."

"Thanks."

When she let him go, Les offered his hand.

"Welcome to the family, Randy. Michelle told us what happened. We don't hold this against you. And you gave us a healthy grandson. We love grandkids."

"Thanks."

He made his way to Michelle and kissed her. She smiled up at him, then took a deep breath.

"Mom. Dad. I hope your plans are flexible. If you can stay around a week, you can be here for our wedding."

"So soon?" Bev said.

"I should have done it as soon as I could answer yes and no questions," Randy replied. "When I got my voice back, I told Michelle we could do it as soon as she was ready. She's had a wedding planner working round the clock so ... we could get married while you're here."

Michelle smiled.

"There are some things money *can* buy. I know the rest of the family will be disappointed, but it's time."

Randy chuckled.

"That's not exactly true. Dad's sending the plane for the rest of the family the day before. So Les, if you need to get home faster, you can fly back."

"Well, now, that's quite an offer."

Michelle looked up at Randy.

"When did you and your dad hatch this?"

"As soon as you picked the date. I called the ranch after your parents left. The rest of your family is already making plans."

She pulled him down for a kiss.

"Thank you."

"There's no reason they can't be here."

"I love you. Show Mom and Dad the house."

"House?" Bev said. "Are you planning to build a house already?"

Randy handed her a magazine, showing a house plan with modifications in blue ink. Les whistled.

"That must be almost as big as your parents' house."

"It covers about the same area, but it's a lot smaller ... because it's only one story."

Bev frowned.

"That's such a big expense for a couple starting out."

"Bev, would it help to know that we won't need a mortgage?"
She stared at him.

"You have that much?"

"I could pay for it without selling my house in Phoenix, which I've put on the market."

"Oh, my. I guess I can't even imagine that."

"So," Les said. "You never have to work another day."

"No. I want to. I've already started learning the publishing business. But it won't be a real demanding job. I'll have plenty of time for my wife and kids."

"Good. First thing's first."

* * *

Michelle and Randy's wedding came off flawlessly in his parents' living room. An impossible timetable became possible by throwing money at the problem. Caterers, decorators, florists, and tailors hired extra people to make it happen.

Rachel served as matron-of-honor, while Carlos drove from Arizona to act as best man, with Sara as flower girl.

Michelle and Randy exited the reception early, leaving Robby with his grandparents for a few hours.

The next day, Les flew home with his sons and several other family members. Bev, her daughters-in-law, and grandchildren waited another day before departing.

Robby began sleeping longer, giving both of his parents a break. Randy smiled at Michelle.

"You don't look so sleep-deprived."

"I was beginning to wonder if those bags under my eyes would ever go away. Probably made great wedding pictures."

"We didn't look so bad that day. Thank God for your mom." He handed her coffee. "Now that you're up, I'll make my morning rounds."

She smiled over her cup.

"You sure you wouldn't rather be a rancher than go off to publish newspapers?"

"I'd love it. But Dad's already claimed that job. He wants me to take over so he can just stay on the ranch. He's earned the right. Even after he retires, I'll probably only go to work three days a week."

"Sounds nice."

He kissed her.

"Be back in an hour or so. Love you, Mrs. Mc Kay."

"I like the sound of that. I love you."

He returned five minutes later, holding a sheet of paper. Michelle felt a chill.

"What's wrong?"

He bit his lip.

"Susan's made her next move."

She shuddered.

"What does it say?"

"It's from Sergio. Says he knows who kidnapped me. Wants me to meet him at the hanger."

"It's a trap."

"I know." He checked his gun. "She won't catch me by surprise this time."

"You're not going."

"She's terrorized me long enough. This ends today."

"I'm calling the FBI."

"Good. Call Dad in twenty minutes. I don't want him walking into a trap."

"You'll be walking into it."

"No. She'll expect me to come on the road. I'll ride Goldie through the trees and come in the back door."

"What should I tell your dad?"

He hesitated.

"The spy has showed himself. Tell him Sergio's involved. He'll find out soon enough about Susan."

Michelle gripped his arm.

"Be careful."

"I will. I won't let her win. We'll never have to worry about her again."

He gave her a long kiss, then left the house, crossing to the horse pasture. She watched him bring Goldie out while she reached for the phone.

XXXV.

When Randy dismounted in the trees a hundred yards behind the hanger, he recognized the disadvantage of riding without tack. Having nothing to tie Goldie, the horse would follow
him. Once he ducked inside the hanger, his horse might give away
his presence.

He detached his holster, then removed his belt. Looping it
around one of Goldie's front legs, he tied it in a knot around the
other leg, forming crude hobbles. Not strong enough for the aver-
age horse, but effective for Goldie.

He left the holster, keeping the automatic ready. In the narrow clearing behind the hanger, he found an unfamiliar car. Susan would be using a rental to cover her tracks.

Only a walk-through door interrupted the back wall of the
hanger. He stole across the clearing and crouched beside the door,
thinking about what lay inside.

Where would I hide if I were planning an ambush? The storage
area above the office? Not enough cover. Inside the twin engine?
Someone would notice the open door. Same with the single engine. The jeep also provided little cover.

No. The piles of tires to the right side of the main door provided the best cover for an ambush. Susan could not see this entrance from that hiding place.

He rotated the knob, hoping for silence. It unlatched with a soft click and he studied what he could see through a two-inch gap. He eased it open until he could fit through, then looked around before proceeding. No sign of Susan.

Then he remembered Sergio. Would he be with her? Had the gardener watched him leave and reported to Susan?

Randy had used caution when he left the house. He had looked specifically for Sergio, seeing no sign of him or his old pickup. And if anyone had warned Susan, she probably would have confronted him by now.

He let his breath out. He had the element of surprise. But would Susan recruit Sergio for the ambush? No. He doubted that Sergio had the nerve to provide more than a set of eyes. Susan did not like loose ends. She may have already eliminated him.

Still crouching, he slid inside, closing the door behind him. Randy scurried under the twin engine plane. With the end of the tire pile visible, he inched along for a better view.

He caught his breath. Susan, gun in hand, almost hidden behind the pile. He could take her from here with a head shot. In the eyes of the law, that would make him no better than her. And he did not want to kill her. He wanted her brought to justice. Still, he doubted that she would surrender without a fight. She had murdered three men. Maybe four.

How can I use my advantage? His eyes settled on a five-foot tall, rolling tool chest, standing in almost a direct line between him and Susan. The metal walls and drawers full of tools would stop her bullets. And provide mobile cover.

He devised a plan, then darted for the tool chest. Susan saw him move and reacted. But by the time she opened fire, the red metal stood between him and her weapon. He nearly slammed into the tool chest. She stopped shooting.

"Give it up, Susan!"

"You wish!"

"You lost your advantage! You didn't surprise me! And I'm not a little kid anymore!"

"So come and get me!"

"I don't want to kill you!"

"Well, there's the difference. I'm looking forward to killing you."

"The FBI's on the way."

"They won't get here before I finish what I came to do."

Randy leaned low against the tool chest, exercising care because of its high center of gravity. If it toppled, he would have no cover. When it began rolling, he pushed harder, gaining momentum.

Susan fired and swore.

With no way to see his target, Randy's aim proved less than accurate, but no less effective. He hit the tires three feet to Susan's right. Like dominos, the entire pile collapsed. She yelped and cursed again. He leaped from cover, gun ready.

The tires had missed only her head. Momentarily stunned, she gasped, then began trying to extricate herself. He could not see her hands, had no idea if she had lost the gun.

"Don't move!"

She pushed a tire off herself.

"I should have smothered you in your crib. But it took me five years to work up the nerve to try to get rid of you."

"Why do you hate me so much?"

"*I* was the heir. It was *my* dream to take over the publishing business. You *stole* that from me. Just because you're male. You didn't even care about it."

"You're right. I didn't care about it. Until I realized that if I didn't, you'd end up with it. And you're way too sick to have that kind of influence."

She called him a filthy name.

"Don't think you've won. I'll make everyone believe you're delusional."

"The FBI is collecting evidence against you now. And how are you going to explain this."

"I can be very convincing."

Susan pushed another tire off. Randy saw the gun.

"Drop it!"

Instead, she swung it toward him. He fired once. Susan groaned and pulled the trigger. The gun discharged into a tire. It fell from her hand as a red stain spread across the front of her blouse.

Randy lowered his weapon, his hand shaking.

Susan coughed up blood. He saw no regret in her eyes. Only hatred. She cursed him, coughed again, and stopped breathing.

Randy drifted outside. Leaning against the door frame, he sank to the concrete apron, letting the gun drop beside him. He hung his head, resting his forearms on his knees.

When the pickup roared to a stop nearby, he barely noticed.

"Randy!" Kendall said. "Are you okay, son?"

He met his father's gaze.

"She's dead. I didn't want to kill her."

"She? Who? Who's dead?"

"Susan. She was behind it all."

"Susan? No. She couldn't hate you that much."

Randy nodded.

"She did, Dad."

Kendall stared at his son, knowing the truth, but not wanting to believe it.

"Where is she?"

"The tires." When his father drifted away, Randy turned his gaze to Sam. "Don't let him touch anything. Call Michelle for me."

Sam nodded and followed Kendall. Randy leaned his head against the wall and closed his eyes. He had no concept of how much time passed.

"Randy."

He looked into Michelle's eyes and fell into her arms, sobbing.

* * *

"How are you, Captain Mc Kay?" Agent Lyons asked.

"Better. I didn't have any nightmares last night. This is harder on my parents. I'd already accepted that my sister was a killer. They have to come to grips with that. They're wondering where they went wrong. The doctor prescribed a sedative for Mom."

"Sometimes, there is no explanation. Her pathological hatred for you made her believe that the end justifies the means. She killed four men without remorse."

"She didn't even show remorse when she knew she was dying. She cursed me with her last breath. Do you think she planned to pin this on Sergio?"

"Yes. She placed his body behind the tires. She shot him with a different gun. Probably intended to make it look like you shot each other."

"Why'd he help her? She wasn't nice to anyone. Why would he want to help her?"

"When we dug deeper, we discovered that his birth certificate was a forgery. He was an illegal alien. His wife admitted that your sister helped him, making it clear that he would owe her. She got him the job with your parents."

"If I'd known that, it would've been easy to pick the spy."

"Of course."

Michelle hugged Randy and asked her question.

"How are her husband and son taking this?"

"Her husband screamed for justice. Claimed you were the villain. She had both of them brainwashed. By the time we confronted him with all the evidence linking her to her accomplices, he looked like he'd seen a ghost. I don't think you need to worry that your brother-in-law will cause you any problems."

"Good," Randy said. "I'm ready to move on. We can do that, can't we? It's over?"

"Yes. I came today to give you my final report. This case is closed."

LaVergne, TN USA
16 December 2009
167261LV00007B/30/P